A Highland Collie

ALBERT PAYSON TERHUNE

A Highland Collie

ORIGINALLY PUBLISHED AS

The Luck of the Laird

Grosset & Dunlap

PUBLISHERS

NEW YORK

As much of my book
as may be worth his approval
is dedicated to

EUGENE F. SAXTON

A Highland Collie

CHAPTER ONE

———

It was a raw February morning in Midwestbury when Rufus G. Belden, one of the two wealthiest and most powerful tycoons of that smoky metropolis, returned home in one of his nastiest tempers. Two Pullman porters, a dining-car waiter and several innocent train passengers had gratuitously experienced his foul mood as he journeyed from New York where he had been attending the annual Westminster Dog Show at Madison Square Garden.

Nor was the drive from the station to the Belden country estate any too pleasant for the family chauffeur, for not only had the great man ignored his pleasant greetings at the train-shed gate, but all the way home the rear-view mirror revealed the master hunched in glowering silence in the back seat. Anyone who knew Rufus G. Belden would have detected behind the lines of sullen rage that marked his fat, heavy face a trace of fear, perhaps even of panic.

His mansion, "Beldencroft," and its two square miles of surrounding domain, was the show place of the state. The house looked like a cathedral whose strabismic designer had studied architecture in ancient Babylon. It was its obese owner's delight.

But Belden's chief pride and joy were centered in the ornate kennels that took up an acre of his landscaped grounds.

Here Rufus G. bred and raised for exhibition some of the most renowned collies in America. Ever it had been his yearning to be known as "The Collie King" as once his life-model, J. Pierpont Morgan, Sr., had been known.

He had succeeded almost according to his dreams. This through no dog-breeding genius of his own, but by reason of great good luck in having the services of one Jamie Mackellar, his soft-spoken little kennel manager of Scottish ancestry.

For years, Jamie's glorious collie, Champion Lochinvar Bobby, had headed the Beldencroft kennels. He had won prize after prize at a hundred dog shows from the Atlantic to the Pacific. But now Lochinvar Bobby was aging. His classic muzzle was silvered. He was taking on flesh. His show days were past. He was living out his last years in retirement as an honored and loved occupant of Jamie Mackellar's snug cottage behind the kennels.

Many another good collie there was at Beldencroft, but none as good as Bobby—none to be relied on to clean up all the best prizes at all the best shows.

Willard Ulrich, the lumber king, had begun to press Belden uncomfortably close for supremacy in the collie world, even as he was challenging Belden's long-undisputed supremacy in Midwestburg's financial and political fields.

For example, at the recent Westminster Dog Show, at New York, Ulrich's three newly imported collies had won with comparative ease over the best dogs from the Beldencroft kennels. Hence the return of Rufus G. Belden today to his manorial acres in such a vile mood.

Out of his limousine he debouched, like a sizzling onion from its shuck skin. Leaving Jamie Mackellar to go to the kennels and see after the welfare of the collies that had come from the show on the same train with Rufus G. and the little manager, the great man strode indoors.

In the front hall he paused in his wrathful progress toward his study. A reluctant half grin replaced his scowl. Light and fast steps were coming down the ugly marble staircase toward him. Then those same steps were carrying across the wide hallway a fluffy and dainty and altogether attractive girl of perhaps twenty.

"Hello, daddy!" she hailed the returned magnate, standing on tiptoe to kiss his florid cheek. "I thought you were going to stay in New York an extra day, to celebrate. We—"

"There wasn't anything to celebrate," grunted Belden, his scowl coming back and driving away the grin his daughter's approach had evoked. "Not a measly thing to celebrate. So Mackellar and I brought the dogs home. Phyll, it was a Waterloo! Ulrich swept the boards. We didn't get a look-in. One 'reserve winners' and a few cheap 'specials.' That was all. Ulrich nabbed 'winners' in both male and female, and 'best of breed,' besides. Everything! He—"

"Poor old daddy!" soothed the girl. "It was putrid hard luck. I'm ever so sorry. But we—"

" 'Putrid hard luck' is a sloppy mild name for it!" stormed Belden in one of the gusts of noisy temper that made him hated by half his world and feared by most of the other half. "It was a damn sight worse than that. I want to know why I'm paying thirty thousand dollars a year for the upkeep and showing of my dogs, if I'm to be licked to a frazzle by a tyro like Willard Ulrich. I mean to know the reason for that, Phyll. Just as I make it a rule to find out where the sagging spot is in any other detail of my business."

"After all," she suggested, with a superiority that was maddening, "a dog show is only just a dog show, and—"

"And a defeat is just as much a defeat at a dog show as at a national convention, and just as tough to swallow. I'm going to put Jamie Mackellar on the carpet, and—"

"No, you're not, daddy!" laughed the girl, speaking tolerantly as to a child in a tantrum. "You know very well you're not. In the first place, Mackellar is the only person in the world, except me, who isn't the least tiny bit afraid of you. And second, because he's the only person on earth you have any respect for—including me. And third, because you know there isn't a better kennel chief in America than he is."

Rufus G. Belden glowered dourly down into his

daughter's laughing face. He knew she was speaking the truth. He depended implicitly on little Mackellar and had boundless confidence in him. Nevertheless, Belden yearned for someone on whom to vent his peevish wrath. Phyllis went on, primly:

"Besides, it's your own fault, your own pigheadedness. Mackellar told you, ages ago, that you needed new blood in the kennels and that the old Beldencroft strain was too closely inbred and that it was wearing out. He said Mr. Ulrich was importing the best dogs in Europe to improve his strain, and he advised you to do it, too. I heard him. And I heard Roy Garth tell you so, too. He—"

"Roy Garth?" snorted Belden, with something of the air of a raging bull that sights at last a red rag for the venting of his temper. "Roy Garth? That mangy little whippersnapper! I'll thank him to keep his asinine opinions to himself, if he wants to hold down his job as my secretary. What does that callow fool know about dogs —or about anything else? Hey? Tell me that! He's—"

"He knows enough about collies to hold a judging license from the American Kennel Club!" spoke up Phyllis, her air of teasing tolerance tinged with sudden warmth. "Jamie Mackellar himself says Roy has as good an eye for the true collie type as anyone he knows. He was brought up among collies. As for his not 'knowing anything else'—well, he knows enough to hold his job as your secretary for two years, when you've always fired every other secretary inside of six months. He's held it without cringing to you, either."

Abruptly Phyllis Belden walked away, her head high, her heels clicking on the slippery floor. Rufus G. stared after her stupidly. Gone was his brief flurry of temper—expelled by what his daughter's temper-flash told him.

It never had occurred to Belden that the feather-souled girl could regard his secretary in any more personal light than she regarded his butler or his housekeeper.

Phyllis had come home to Beldencroft, from finishing school and from a year in Europe, ten months earlier. She had found Roy Garth installed in the garish house as her father's secretary. From the first, girl and youth had gotten on well together. Belden had been mildly pleased with their jolly talk. It had brought a brightness into the gloomy splendor of Beldencroft.

Indeed, Rufus G. had admired secretly the education and the travel lore of both—Rufus G. whose workaday life had begun before he had been able to finish grammar school. But not for an instant had it struck him, until now, that when a young and lively and clever man and maid are thrown much together in a lonely household, mere acquaintanceship may refuse to continue on as mere acquaintanceship. The sudden suspicion jarred Belden.

Perhaps he might have noticed earlier the direction wherein Phyllis's fancy was drifting, had not a false clue thrown him far off the scent. He hated Willard Ulrich, his business and dog-show rival, with all the concentrated virulence of a self-willed, violent man. But for some time it had been very apparent that the hatred and rivalry were not to be carried on into the next generation.

The lumber monarch's only son, young Brant Ulrich, had taken to calling often on Phyllis Belden, and the girl had not seemed to find his attentions irksome. After the first visit, Belden had had one of his liveliest tantrums. Loudly and profanely he had forbidden Phyllis to allow the son of his enemy to set foot in Beldencroft again. He had forbidden her to speak to the youth, should they chance to meet elsewhere. Phyllis had heard out the roaring tirade. Then she had smiled sweetly and said:

"Your nose wabbles ever so funnily when you bellow, daddy! I wish you could see it. Sometime you must try to have a tantrum in the looking-glass. And— Oh, you were talking about Brant Ulrich, weren't you, dear old thing? Well, of course I'm going to keep right on seeing him any time I want to. You'll remember that, won't you? Yes? That's a good obedient daddy!"

Had any employee or friend—had anyone but his hopelessly spoiled daughter flouted the express commands of Rufus G., certain punishment would have followed with thunderbolt swiftness and devastation. As it was, a prolonged scene of some intensity ensued, leaving the situation just where Phyllis wanted it left. Brant Ulrich continued to call. Belden did his fuming privily, and he stored up direful explosives against the dreaded time when Brant might present his claims for the post of future son-in-law.

This shift to Garth lifted a dreary weight of apprehension from Belden's soul—or from the place where his soul should have been. But the weight was replaced at once by a rankling that was scarcely more comfortable. Rufus G. had built a huge fortune from nothing. One day this hoard must belong to his adored daughter. In daydreams he had imagined her as sharing it with a British duke or at the very least with some financial and social luminary of her own country. He had not piled up this fortune for a mere secretary to enjoy.

As between Roy Garth and Ulrich, there could be no doubt of Belden's preference. But he wanted neither as a son-in-law. He liked young Garth. The boy had promise and brains and grit. Rightly started, he might go far. But Phyllis was for some superman of wealth or fashion or rank who already had gone far.

As ever, when perplexity gripped him, Belden jammed on his hat and went forth to the kennels to hunt up Jamie Mackellar. He had grown to place queer reliance in the little Scot's shrewd common sense and in his simple methods of solving knotty problems. Hence, Belden had formed a habit of consulting Jamie even on affairs that were far outside the kennel chief's province. Often he took the Scot's wise advice in such matters. Oftener he had cause to regret not taking it.

He found Jamie, this morning, still clad in the ill-fitting black diagonal-cloth suit and the black stiff derby which were Mackellar's idea of gala attire. He was supervising the transfer from crates to kennel yards of the four top-notch Beldencroft collies which had made the fruitless journey to New York.

"I rubbed the powdered naphthalene into them and

sponged their mouths and their pads with alcohol, right after the show," he was saying to one of the kennelmen. "Now just be putting them in their houses where they can rest quiet after their hantle of railroad riding, and give each one of them a big tablespoonful of castor oil. Best to be sure than sorry, with all the lot of distemper that's going through the shows lately. They— Were you looking for me, sir?" he broke off as Belden appeared in the doorway.

"Yes," answered Rufus G., curtly. "Come over to your cottage. I want a chat with you."

On Jamie's arrival, a few minutes earlier, a bronze giant of a collie had disregarded the stiffness of oncoming age and had rushed forth from the cottage to fling himself screechingly upon his week-absent master. Jamie himself had returned the greeting with little less enthusiasm, heedless of the myriad muddy paw-streaks with which the dog was adorning the hallowed black diagonal Sunday suit. For this was Jamie's loved collie, Lochinvar Bobby, his housemate and chum.

Bobby had stuck close to Mackellar's heels as the manager moved about the kennels. Now, with nothing of his recent fervor, but with grave friendliness, the collie advanced to salute Belden. Rufus G. laid a hamlike hand in clumsy caress on Bobby's head, then set off with Jamie to the cottage behind the kennels.

Presently Belden was installed in front of a sputtering hearth fire, in a disreputable easy chair that grumbled beneath his ponderous weight. Jamie perched himself on the tiny sitting room's next most comfortable chair, while Lochinvar Bobby curled up on the rug, contentedly, at his master's feet. Followed a moment of embarrassed silence. Then, abruptly, Belden plunged midway into the errand that had brought him hither.

"Mackellar," he said, "barring that time last year when you went back to see your folks in Scotland, you've had your eyes on everything that's gone on here at Beldencroft. I've watched you, and I know. Those blinky blue Scotch eyes of yours have got a way of not seeming to see anything, but there's precious little they don't register."

He paused. Mackellar shuffled his feet and observed, as in some doubt:

"Thanking you kindly for the compliment, sir, if that's how it's meant. But just what does it lead up to? I don't speir you came all the way down here, the minute you're home again, simply to say polite things to me—things that you could have said any time this past week. I take it something has come up since you got back. But what it's got to do with my eyes—"

"If you'll stop babbling, man, you'll find out!" growled Belden.

Meekly Jamie held his peace, looking mild inquiry at his fidgety employer, who seemed in no haste to begin. Clearing his throat at last, Rufus G. demanded, lamely:

"What do you think of Garth?"

"Why, I've told you more'n once that I like him fine!" replied Jamie. "He's a nice upstanding young chap, every way. He's square and he's clever. He's got brains, for all he's so young. Not a genius, as a body might say, but a good sensible lad. And then it's a joy to see such an athletic body as his is and to see the way he treats it. They tell me he is about the best all-rounder they've got, down to the Midwestburg Athletic Club—unless maybe it's young Mr. Brant Ulrich. Good at boxing and wrestling and fencing he is, they say, and a snappy sprinter, too, and nice with the oars. As to his brains, you're the best judge of them. I'm figgering he must have some, or you'd never have kept him on so long."

Purposely the little man was stretching out his answer, and there was a malicious glint in his mild blue eyes as he noted how inattentively his questioner was following his words. Indeed, except for a glower at Jamie's willful mention of Brant Ulrich, Belden seemed to have heard none of the eulogy.

Belatedly aware that Mackellar had lapsed into silence, Belden asked with explosive suddenness:

"Do you think he and my daughter are in love with each other?"

Jamie's face stiffened. Behind the mild eyes glinted something like blue ice.

"It's not for me to dictate your themes for funny jokes, sir," he said, coldly. "But if I may make so free as to say it, that's not quite the kind of jest I'd have thought you'd crack with an employee."

"I'm not joking," snapped Belden. "And you know damn well I'm not. You're trying to snub me, and it's a measly impertinence. I asked you if you think Garth and my daughter are in love with each other. You'd know, if anyone would. You see everything. I want an answer. I'm entitled to it. Not as your boss, but as your friend. Speak up!"

"Mr. Belden," said Jamie, ice still in eye and tone, "there is something like a furlong of lawn between the kennels and your house. My duties lie at the kennels and not one inch beyond them. There's more than a furlong between my job and your right to assume that I'd play the spy by watching anything here that comes outside the square and angle of my own work. That's all the answer there is, sir. And—"

"Mackellar," urged Belden, genuine worry in his fat voice, "I told you I was asking you this question as a friend, not as a boss. There's only you I can come to in this. It's bothering me. I'm asking you to help me out."

"And maybe help a clean lad out of a good job, sir?" queried Mackellar.

Belden winced, his muscles tautening.

"You've given me the answer," he said. "Thanks."

"By your leave, I've done nothing of the kind," disclaimed Mackellar, in distress. "At least—"

"At least you don't want to make Garth risk his job by telling me it's true," supplemented Belden. "I understand. I must have been wearing my eyes in my shoes, not to have noticed it. But you're off about one thing. I'm not going to fire him. If she wants him, I know her well enough and I know myself well enough to know I'll end up by letting her have him. It doesn't taste extra well in my mouth, though it's fifty times better than if it was Ulrich. If I can find a way to smash it, without letting her know, I'll—"

"Mr. Belden," pleaded Jamie, in dire embarrassment, "you're riled, just now. When you quiet down you'll kick yourself for talking about your own daughter's affairs with a kennelman. Suppose we drop it?"

"Not till you give me the advice I came here for," refused Belden.

"You've just given it to yourself, sir," answered Jamie, "when you said you'd likely let her have her own way. And by the bye," he added with elephantine change of subject, "I meant to tell you Stansfield says that when he was in England he saw the litter brother of Mr. Ulrich's winning dog—the one that got 'best of breed' at Madison Square Garden this week. He says it's pretty near as good as the Ulrich dog. I was wondering if maybe you'd care to cable over and buy it. Perhaps I might be able to condition it and get it into shape to—"

"To get us beaten by Ulrich again?" snarled Rufus G. "Thanks. Nothing doing."

But his grievance at the dog-show defeat had switched him momentarily from the theme of Phyllis, as Jamie had intended it should.

"We'll have to get some new collie blood, somewhere or other, sir," insisted Mackellar, "just like I've been telling you. Our own strain is worn too thin. We want an outsider or two. If—"

"But we don't want a dog that will be 'almost' good enough," argued Belden. "I'm sick of having dogs 'almost' good enough to beat Ulrich. I want something that will sweep the show circuit, the way old Lochinvar Bobby, here, used to. There must be some such dog somewhere. I'd give ten thousand dollars today to find him."

"In all my days," ruminated Mackellar, "I've seen only one collie that had better show points than Bobby, here, and I'm apologizing to Bobby for saying so. But it's true. Last year it was I ran across him, when I went back to the old country to see the folks. He—"

"And you never told me! You knew I wanted a super-collie. You saw one and you never even—"

"What would have been the use, sir? All the cash in the mint wouldn't have bought him. Else I'd have told you, right off. As it was, I hated to admit I'd ever seen old Bobby's equal. He—"

"Where did you see him?"

"At Thross, sir. Thross. The village where my folks live and where my folks have lived since before the days when the first Jamie—only the name was Hamish, then —when the first Hamish Mackellar was head shepherd to him they call 'King Macbeth' in the stage play—and to his son, Hamish MacBheathaig."

"Does this wonderful dog belong to your folks over there?"

"Losh! A collie of the Harailt line belong to a Mackellar? Syne ye'll be asking do my folks own the Koh-inoor diamond, and do they drink tea with King George! Why, sir, those dogs, from Harailt down, have belonged to the MacBheathaigs, as the chief's family called itself then; the 'Macbeaths,' as they call themselves now. There's an old legend about the first Harailt bringing good luck to old King Macbeth's son, and a prophecy-like that the chief's family luck will only last while there's dogs of Harailt's race left in the castle."

Belden chuckled in high disdain.

"Laugh if you like to, sir," went on Jamie, unoffended. "Here in the middle of your brand-new American continent anyone can laugh at old legends and at old prophecies, because folk think there's no legends or mysteries here to laugh at. (Which same there *are*.) But up in the age-old Hielands too many queer things have happened to make any Scotsman laugh when he hears of a family prophecy."

"Then I'm glad I live in a country where that kind of 'queer things' can't happen," scoffed Belden, crankily glad to vent some of his ill-humor in the belittling of his kennel manager's homeland traditions. "In America, thank the Lord, nothing happens without a common-sense reason for it. We—"

"Quite!" assented Mackellar, with an exaggeration of his wonted meekness. "There's many such another thing happening here in your blind America, every day; as much as ever such things happened in the old-time Hielands—things that wise men like yourself would be graciously pleased to call 'rank insanity' if the things were pointed out to you. But, somehow, they keep on happening just the same. We poor superstitious old Scots used to harken to such omens and the like, and we tried to profit by them. You all-wise Yankees—saving your presence, sir—you laugh and call it insane nonsense. In that way you think you prove that all superstition is silly. You could do the same thing about lightning and earthquakes, but you couldn't laugh them away. And you can't laugh away a hundred things the good Lord allows to happen and that we up-to-date humans haven't any logical name or reason for. You can call them 'superstition.' But that doesn't keep them from happening. Shall we let it go at that, sir? 'Tis not a theme I enjoy gassing on, with a man that's so much wiser than I am. We were speaking about the collie dog over at Thross, and the—"

"And the hand-painted fake about his carrying his master's luck around with his own fleas," supplemented Belden. "If he's half what you say he is, I want him. And no cock-and-bull legend is going to stop me, either. As to this luck yarn—"

He paused, belatedly noting that Mackellar did not enjoy the slurs on his Highland beliefs and that presently he might show overt resentment. Jamie set his jaw stolidly for an instant, while he warred with a craving to speak right frankly to his fat overlord. Then choking down the temptation, he resumed:

"Anyhow, true or a fake, there's not a soul at Thross, from the Macbeath down, who doesn't believe it. So you see what chances a man would have to buy a dog that means the Luck of the Laird. Besides, there's only this one young collie left, now, of all Harailt's long line. So the Macbeath would be guarding him ten times as much as ever. And, apart from the legend, young Stirling is well worth the guarding. Man, sir, but he's the best collie my two eyes ever had the luck to rest on! There's nothing here or in Great Britain can touch him for perfect show points. And he's a fine sheep-herder, too."

With half-shut eyes, Belden sat in silence. He knew that Mackellar was not given to gushing about any dog's excellence. Moreover, he knew there was no dog judge anywhere with better knowledge of a show collie's points than the mild-eyed little Scot. If Mackellar said this Highland dog was the best in the world, then the dog was the best in the world. Belden's eyes opened again and fixed themselves on his kennel manager.

"When you speak of 'the Macbeath,'" said he, "I take it you mean the present chief. When you came back last fall, you told me how miserably poor his Thross village is, from the chief down. That means they would do pretty much anything for money. Mackellar, I want you to take the next boat to Europe. I want you to go to Thross and offer Macbeath anything up to ten thousand dollars for this Stirling dog you've been telling me about. Tell him it's the highest price ever paid for a collie. Croker paid as much for a bulldog once, and they say Untermeyer paid six thousand five hundred for Squire of Tytton, the best collie of his time. I'll pay ten thousand for Stirling. Tell the chief so. I want that dog. . . .

Well?" as Jamie sat open-mouthed. "What do you say?"

"I say, *no*, sir!" returned Jamie, finding his voice at last, with a gulp. "And I say it good and loud. Why, if a mere Mackellar should go to the Macbeath and have the insolence to try to buy a Harailt collie, he'd be lucky to get away with a whole skin. It'd be *lèse majesté*. I would be on a fool's errand. For that matter, anyone would be. He might not come out of it alive if the Laird should get angry enough to stir up the clan against him."

"But—"

"Over there, sir, up in that wild part of the Hielands, there's plenty of men still who would obey their chief if he told them to step down to Windsor and pull King George's nose. It'd be a fool's errand and a cruel dangerous one at that, to go to the Macbeath in his own castle and ask him to sell his last collie for American cash."

With a sharp gesture of one big hand Belden checked the horrified flow of talk. Again the magnate's head was on his breast and his eyes were closed. Rufus G.'s worst enemy never denied the swift and brilliant inspirations which made Belden feared by his competitors. He was in the clutch of such an inspiration now. Half inaudibly he began to mumble:

"He'd think it was the chance of his life—chance to make good with me—chance to get her when he comes back. . . . He's young. He'd be up on his toes in such a job. I could make it look to him as if it was his life opportunity. . . . There's an off chance he might get the dog, at that. Youth can do a lot, these days. And—he'd be out of the way for perhaps six months or so. Out of the way! Lots can happen here in six months. Or Macbeath might —might— It'll either solve the problem or else it'll put things off indefinitely. . . . Yes, he's the man!"

"If you're still hinting," observed Jamie, who had caught scarce one word in five of the muttered speech— "if you're still hinting I'm the man to go to Thross and maybe be killed trying to—"

"I'm not thinking of you, you poor craven!" yelled Belden, joyously. "I'm thinking of—Garth!"

CHAPTER TWO

LATE that afternoon, Roy Garth came out of his employer's fifty-by-forty private study—a sumptuously grim apartment which blended all the best features of a morgue and a baronial hall—with his hands full of answered letters and his wontedly alert face blank with foolish joy. He deposited the letters in the hall mail bag and made his way to the music room, whence issued peals of vigorous piano notes that were fairly recognizable as the Grieg "Spring Song," albeit played with more than a suggestion of jazziness.

Rufus G. Belden's secretary was square-built and twenty-six. Short, rather than of hero stature, he had a stocky breadth of shoulder and depth of chest which went well with his wolf-lean flanks and compact girth.

There was little more of the story-book hero in his face than in his figure. His hair was reddish and curly. His light eyes were redeemed from mediocrity by a levelness of gaze and by an impish glint of fun behind them. His mouth was large; his nose slightly tiptilted. He had the square and jutting lower jaw of the conventional prize fighter.

At first glance there was more of the professional athlete about his aspect than of the student or secretary. Athletics in almost every form, from fencing to football, had been his life hobby.

Just now, as he tracked down the jazzful Grieg music to its source, his face had neither mischief nor sternness in it, but the aforesaid happy blankness and a wistfully eager smile.

Phyllis Belden looked up from her conscientious rendering of Grieg to see the secretary come into the music room in whirlwind fashion.

"Phyll!" he exclaimed, breaking unceremoniously on her playing. "Phyll! Listen, dear! I've got my chance. I've *got* it. The kind of knight-errant chance that comes to story-book secretaries who go daffy over their bosses' daughters. I'm going over to Scotland. I'm going over there right away. It's a black and solemn secret, and it's my *chance*. Your dad said so himself. He's been telling me about it for an hour. And all the time I was crazy to sneak away and tell you. He—"

"And now that you've 'sneaked away' and spoiled my 'Spring Song' crescendo and gotten me all excited," suggested Phyllis, wholly unimpressed, "why not stop making funny static sounds and looking like the First Conspirator, and tell me what it's about? All I get of it is that you're going to Scotland. That means you're going away from *me*. I've gotten rather used to you, and it isn't good news that you're going. I'm afraid I shall miss you, just a very little bit. . . . No, I don't want to be kissed! I want to be *told*. Now, then!"

Blurtingly, boyishly, Garth began his tale of the super-collie far up in the wildest Scottish Highlands, and of the tradition that the dog brought luck to his master's house, and of the myriad difficulties in the way of buying him and of Belden's obsessed craving to own the wonderful animal.

"He says I'm the only man on earth that he'd trust with such a mission," continued Garth. "Lord! I never heard your dad throw such praise into anyone as he threw into me. According to him, I've got miraculous gifts for diplomacy, and he has faith I can succeed in this impossible stunt. He made *me* have faith in it, too, before he was through telling me about it. I honestly believe I can do it, Phyll. If I don't—"

An elaborate yawn from his sweetheart interrupted the eager recital. It was an artistic yawn, wholly artificial, as Roy knew. Yet it checked the current of his rhapsody.

"I think," she said, plaintively—"I *think* I never heard of anything more thrillingly dramatic. You are going all the way to Scotland and buy a dog and bring him home. What could be grander? I don't wonder you're so stirred up. I can't imagine anything more flamingly heroic, except perhaps to be sent to the corner butcher shop for a five-pound porterhouse steak. Perhaps, if you bring the dog home safely, daddy will promote you to taking in the milk in the morning. . . . And you call it a 'deed of knight errantry'!"

"You don't understand," he urged. "Or maybe I told it clumsily. The boss says there will be need of all the diplomacy I've got, and maybe all the pluck and the strength I've got, too. He says there's liable to be all kinds of ructions. But I hadn't reached the best part of the yarn when you got sarcastic and spoiled it all. I—"

"Oh, there's more to it?" she queried with an infuriating show of pleased politeness. "There's an even greater climax? Dear, if you tell me dad is going to commission you to go to a bird-and-animal store and buy a ferocious Maltese kitten, I don't think I can bear it. It would be too much life-and-death risk for you. No man ought to be sent on such hazardous errands. Volunteers ought to be called for. If—"

Quietly Roy Garth stooped and picked up the laughing girl bodily in his arms. With no effort at all he seated her on the high mantelshelf, six feet above the floor, heedless of the tattoo which her small sharp toes were beating against him, as well as of her furious demands to be set down.

"Now, then," he said, sternly, stepping back and surveying her as she raged helplessly on her lofty perch—"now you'll listen to me, you—you wretched little tease! You ought to be stood in the corner. But there aren't any corners to this egg-shaped room, so the mantel is next best. There you'll stay till you're good again. And meantime you'll listen to the best part of my news."

Phyllis was scowling down at him with all the murderous ferocity of a month-old Persian cat. But at heart she was adoring the man. It was this calm physical perfection of his strength which first had attracted her to

Garth; this and his unexpected deeds of mischief, such as lifting her to a seat whence she could not possibly get back to the floor without his help.

Even as she raged at him she could feel in retrospect the thrill of his arms lifting her so high and so easily, and the queer effrontery of the deed. Presently she ceased to upbraid him and to demand release from her perch. At once Garth took up the thread of his narrative.

"Your father told me frankly that if I can't pull this deal off for him, he won't need me any longer as a secretary. He—"

"The brute!" flashed Phyllis, forgetful of her own grievance. "I'll see he changes his mind about that, if—"

"He won't. And I don't expect him to. In fact, I agreed to it. Because he told me—at least he hinted it strongly enough—that if I succeed in this quest—well, he didn't say it in so many words, but then he didn't need to. I understood."

"Understood what?"

"We were mistaken, you and I, when we thought we'd been able to keep him from finding out about us. He didn't put that in so many words, either. But he let me understand that he knew, and that he won't raise any great objections to it, if I win out on this Scotch mission. Honestly, he did, sweetheart. That's the 'great' part of my news. Isn't it glorious?"

"I—I can't possibly kiss you from way up here!" cried the girl, infected by his enthusiasm almost as much as by his tidings. "Lift me down, you clumsy piano mover.

Lift me down. . . . No, not *all* the way down; just far enough down to— There! Daddy *is* a dear, after all. Isn't he?"

Drawn by their voices, Rufus G. Belden had strolled from his study as far as the tapestry curtains that shut off the music room from the hallway. Now he turned and walked noiselessly back to his desk.

Rufus G. was smiling. It was not a pretty smile. No mushy idealist could possibly have construed it into a smile of sympathy in his daughter's happiness.

Belden had made many of his sixty million dollars by dint of a genius for postponing unpleasant crises and by the really inspired way in which he improved his time during such periods of postponement.

Today he was well satisfied. Not only was he getting an ineligible suitor out of the way for a number of months, during which months he could trust to his own cleverness to break up the match, but he had inspired the poor dupe with a fiery determination to get for him the marvelous Macbeath collie for whose possession Rufus G. yearned so keenly.

More than once, as Belden knew from experience, a fanatic resolve to win has proven itself worth more, in a physical or a mental fight, than all the crafty diplomacy in existence. Brighter and brighter seemed Belden's prospects for losing his daughter's wooer and for winning a grand dog. He felt he had achieved a fair day's work.

At dusk, Garth sauntered down to the Midwestburg Athletic Club for his daily hour of strenuous exercise before dinner. He was in a finer glow, as he entered the club gym, than any mere exercise could give him. To all men is it given at times to feel that strange exaltation of spirit and of body. Unluckily, to few of them is it given to know that such unnatural exaltation usually precedes a smashing fall.

Life's road lay dazzlingly clear before Garth. He was engaged to a girl who infatuated him to the point of idiocy. And now he had a chance, by dint of his own prowess, to achieve a mission which should place her within his reach. Not all the musty Macbeaths in Scotland could prevent him from triumphing in his quest. He was tensely and joyously certain of that.

Stripping, he hammered the fight-weight punching bag for three minutes, then spent another ten minutes in shadow boxing and with the chest weights, while he waited for a strapping assistant instructor to put on the gloves with him for two fast rounds. Next, without rest, he commandeered the same instructor for a ten-minute wrestle on the mat.

Still glowing and untired, he slipped into a padded plastron jacket and flannel trousers and into tennis shoes, and went across the hall to the *salle d'armes* for a five-minute bout with the broadswords. His day's athletic work ended, he sought the pool and a fast swim before rubbing down and dressing.

As he was crossing the clubhouse's outer hall on the way to the street, he encountered three men who were walking toward the gym. Two of the trio would not have caused a second glance anywhere. They were of the type which seems destined to make up the personnel of a crowd and whose representatives, in olden plays, used to be characterized as "First and Second Citizen" or as "Confused Noise Without."

But the third would have attracted notice in whatever company he might have been. Strikingly handsome in blond Norse viking fashion, he stood perhaps six-feet-two in his stockings. He had steam-radiator shoulders and a ballet-girl waist. In build he was an almost perfect copy of the ancient super-athletes which Canova loved to model in snowy marble for the envy of lesser men.

Had Brant Ulrich met Garth elsewhere than in this club of theirs, Roy would have contrived not to en-counter the blond giant's eye. But here they were rival athletes, close competitors with gloves and with broad-swords and on the mat. From sheer sportsmanship, Garth could not walk past a rival athlete, in this place of their rivalry, without a nod.

Yet he made the nod as stiff and as impersonal as he could. Ulrich returned the salutation with a nod if pos-sible slighter and stiffer, then passed on. As he went, the big man said something to his two companions. All three laughed loudly.

Roy Garth stalked out into the street, red with an-noyance, and his exultant glow chilled for the moment. There are few things more vexing than to know or to guess that one is the theme for such laughter as Ulrich's two companions had lavished upon their friend's low-spoken witticism. Garth knew well they were laughing at him. Childishly he yearned to go back to the three and demand explanation or to call Brant Ulrich noisily to personal account.

Then, squaring his shoulders, he dismissed the foolish temptation and hurried on. He could afford to let Ulrich laugh, Roy told himself; Ulrich was openly and hopelessly in love with the glorious girl who had given her heart to Garth. Little enough had Brant to laugh about! Roy had beaten him in fair contest for Phyllis's love. Penniless and without prospects he had won her, against the Apollo-like Ulrich's social leadership and his millions of dollars. Roy had beaten him, even as Roy intended to beat him in next week's boxing and fencing tournament at the club.

At that thought, Garth was aware of a twinge of disappointment. Long and hard had he been training for the tournament. And now he must forfeit its best events to Ulrich. Roy was due to sail for Scotland within a week. Already the wires had been set to work in reserving his passage on the first available boat.

With Roy absent, Ulrich assuredly would win both the heavyweight boxing cup and the broadsword trophy. Well, let him win them! Roy would be winning something a billion times more precious. Time enough to compete for mere athletic cups in older years, when his life's happiness should have been won.

Blithely, Garth made his swinging way up the steep hill on whose crest Beldencroft overlooked the soot and roar of the city. He dressed for dinner, looking forward to a wonderful evening with Phyllis.

But as he was rising from the dinner table, Belden said to him in unwonted courtesy:

"Sorry to give you another three hours of hustling, Roy, on top of a busy day. But those C. G. & X. reports came while you were out. They've got to be tabulated and boiled down before the board meeting tomorrow. That means a kind of wakeful evening for you and me, I guess. Suppose we start in right away? We'll get through before midnight, then."

With a whimsically tragic glance at Phyllis as he passed by the music room where she sat waiting for him, Roy followed his obese overlord into the study. Nor did it add to his concentration and peace of mind when, an hour later, through the study doorway, he saw Brant Ulrich ushered across the hall toward the little music room.

Still, what was one evening in a whole lifetime? Cheerily, he asked himself the question, more than once, as he bent above the reams of dry railroad reports on his desk. Luckily for himself, there was no soothsayer to answer his optimistic query and to tell him that the events of this one evening were to be the more or less direct cause of turning his entire future upside down.

It was not until late the next day that Garth had his first inkling of the seemingly innocuous evening's dire results. He was on his way back to Beldencroft from the athletic club. As he turned into the grounds a wizened little figure confronted him.

Jamie Mackellar had been standing there in the chill and damp for the best part of half an hour, to intercept the secretary. Roy greeted the Scotsman in gay friendliness. Jamie made no reply to the hail, but said, gloomily:

"Come down to the cottage with me a few minutes, Mr. Garth. I'll not detain you long."

Garth glanced at his watch.

"I haven't much more than time to dress for dinner, Jamie," said he. "Will it do if I drop in on you before bedtime or tomorrow morning? I—"

"No," answered Jamie, firmly, "it will not. Come."

He led the way without further word. Nor did he speak again until he and the puzzled youth were in Mackellar's snug living room. Lochinvar Bobby got up from the hearth and trotted over to his beloved master. For once, Jamie ignored the wagging tail and the inquiring muzzle.

The old dog found more cordial return for his greeting from Garth. The secretary was one of the very few humans whom Bobby had honored with his friendship. Roy had a way with all animals, and he understood collies better than it is given to the average fancier to understand them.

"Well, then," asked Garth, as Jamie stood on the ragged hearth rug, glowering moodily up at him, "what's all the mystery? Speak up, won't you? I'll get a worse glower than yours if I'm twelve seconds late for dinner. So—"

"You're full due to get that same glower, whether

you stay to listen to me or not," was Jamie's cryptic reply. "That's why I was waiting out yon for you. Hech,
but the wet ground was no grand help to my rheumatics,
either," he added, addressing Bobby rather than the guest.

"I'm mighty sorry, Jamie. What's—?"

"Mr. Garth," interrupted Jamie, rapping out his words
with unaccustomed sharpness, "this afternoon the bench
show committee of the Midwestburg Kennel Club held
its meeting, to line up matters for the April show. I'm on
that committee. So is Jonas Dod."

"Jonas Dod?" echoed Roy, perplexed. "Who is—? Oh,
he's Willard Ulrich's new kennel manager, isn't he? The
one he imported from England? I think you told me
about him. He—"

"And I'm going to tell you a wee peckle more about
him. He and I both happened to get to the meeting on
time. That means we both got there a hantle of minutes
before anyone else did, such being the kittle-kattle ways
of bench show committees. Likewise, Jonas Dod had
been to lunch with some English friends and they had
smuggled a mort of Scots whiskey into the country with
them. Which means that Jonas Dod was more than mod-
erate drunk by the time I forgathered with him."

Garth glanced furtively again at his watch.

"He was talky drunk," went on Jamie, unhurried.
"Worse, he was braggy drunk. The braggier he got, the
looser his brain got, till at last it fell wide open. He
bragged how his boss's dogs had beat us at Westminster.
Then he bragged how his boss was going to spike us

everywhere with a collie named Stirling, that young Mr. Brant Ulrich is going to post over to Thross after, by the first boat he can catch."

Garth's firm jaw dropped slack. He stared wordlessly.

"Shame to me that I listened," continued Jamie, "and muckle shame to me that I led him on, as crafty-like as I could! But I did it for the boss who pays me my salt and for a babbly lad named Garth that I've a bit liking for. And this is what I got out of the poor gabby drunken loon:

"Mr. Brant Ulrich calls on a young lady, last evening. She forgets that her father's interests are her own interests and that her father's enemies should also be her enemies—not that I'm presuming to blame her, me being old-fangled and not smart enough to fathom the new generation—and she tells all about your trip to Scotland and what it's for and that I said Stirling is the finest show collie on earth today.

"So Mr. Brant Ulrich posts home to his dad with the story. You know as well as I do how keen Mr. Willard Ulrich always is to get the best of the boss. Well, here was a chance for him to cut in ahead and buy the collie that Mr. Belden is honing for, and likewise to beat us unmercifully at every show for years to come.

"You'll maybe remember that Mr. Belden said nobody but you and me and him was to get a breath of news about your trip, just for fear of some such very thing as the Ulrichs are aiming to do. Now, somebody told Miss Phyllis. *I* didn't. This noon when Mr. Belden was going through the kennels with me he told me he hadn't spoke a word of it to anyone but yourself and that you were too level-headed to blab. Mr. Garth, that seems to put the leak pretty square up to *you*. Now, what is to do about it?"

It was a long speech for the taciturn little Scot. Indeed, it had quite winded him. For a moment after he fell silent, Roy Garth spoke no word.

The secretary's shimmery air castles lay in heaps around him. Gone was his glad exultation. Gone, too, were his hopes of a triumph which should win Phyllis for him. His chance was lost—the chance on which he had staked his life's golden future. Doubtless, too, his job was forfeit.

But all this was as nothing to him, nor did its details so much as flit through his tortured mind. His soul was writhing in red torment over the knowledge that the girl he adored had betrayed him. Not merely that she had betrayed her own father's interests, but had betrayed her lover's sacred confidence—the confidence on which depended their love.

It had not occurred to Garth to bind her to silence, nor to suppose her father did not wish her told. He had been certain she could not help keeping the great secret inviolate. He would not have insulted her by warning her not to speak of it. And now she had betrayed him— betrayed him to the man he detested and who detested him!

Mackellar was speaking again. As from a long distance, Roy heard him say:

"I suppose it was my duty to go to the boss with this.

But—well, I like you, lad, and I know full well what follies a boy in love will do and say. So I waited for you, instead. I can find it in my conscience to say nothing at all to Mr. Belden. But I had to warn *you* that your errand, over yon in Thross, will be fifty times as hard and dangerous as ever it would have been if the Ulrichs had not known of this. And it was plenty hard and dangerous, as it was. Young Mr. Brant Ulrich will have all the money and all the influence behind him that his dad can supply. Yes, and if rumors don't lie, he has no love for you and it will pleasure him to thwart you and crush you. Lad, you're going barefoot and blindfold into a rattlesnake den! If you come out of it safe, or even alive, you'll be playing in rare bright luck. I wanted to warn you. I'll make it no worse by telling Mr. Belden. But maybe you will be sensible and give over the crazy idea of going to Thross at all, now. Mr. Belden needn't know. I—I'll do more: I'll tell him I just had a letter that said the wonderful dog has died or something. Then—"

Garth caught the Scot by the thin shoulders and shook him. Bobby glared up fiercely, then wagged his plumed tail in relief.

"Jamie!" groaned the miserable secretary. "I'm obliged to you. But I'm going to Thross, just the same. Not that there's likely to be any reward in it for me, the way things have turned out. But because I couldn't look at myself in the shaving glass again, if I didn't. I'll go there, if I have to go on my own hook. And now, the first thing is for me to tell Mr. Belden what you've told me, and to take my medicine—or as much of it as I can swallow."

"You'll not—there is no need—"

"There is all the need in the world—unless I want to grow a beard. I told you I want to be able to look at myself in the shaving glass. Good-by, Jamie. And bless you for your kindness to me!"

Dully, almost stumblingly, Roy made his way to the house and to his employer's study. Rufus G. was not there. He had gone upstairs to dress for dinner. But Phyllis was rummaging sacrilegiously in one of the hallowed desk drawers as Garth entered the vast room. At sight of Roy, she called across to him:

"Where do you and daddy keep the special-delivery stamps? I've been looking for five minutes for— Why, what on earth is the matter, darling? You look as if Edgar Allan Poe had written you!"

CHAPTER THREE

———

GARTH had stepped into the radius of lamplight and she saw his haggard face. Now, lifelessly he spoke, making no move toward Phyllis as she came running up to him in pretty anxiety.

"Did you tell Brant Ulrich about my trip to Scotland?" he asked, heavily, with no hint of accusal or of anger in his dead voice. "Did you tell him I was going there to get a dog for your father that could win against the best in the Ulrich kennels? Did you tell him where I hoped to find that dog? Did—"

"I certainly did!" she made instant and gay reply. "But I don't see why it makes you look so tragic, dear. I hadn't meant to say anything to you about it, because I knew it would distress you. Not my telling him that rigmarole, of course, but because I'd have to tell you I had told him about—us."

"Us?" he babbled, dazed.

"He came here last evening," explained Phyllis, slipping her hand into Roy's unresponding palm. "He—he asked me to marry him. I knew he was going to. But I thought I could get rid of him without much trouble.

I couldn't. He made a *horrid* scene, Roy. To shut him up, I had to tell him I was in love with you. Then he lost his head, and—and, oh, he said vilely mean things about you and about how little you amount to or ever will amount to!

"I could have killed him. But I made up my mind he should know how splendidly worth-while you are and that you *do* amount to something. So I told him you were so important that daddy was sending you on a mission he wouldn't trust anyone else with—the hardest and most ticklish mission any man could go on; and that he wouldn't do that unless you were gorgeously clever. You *are* clever, darling, you know."

As Garth's face had remained dead white and wretched and as his hand failed to respond to her tender clasp, the girl was seeking to flatter him out of his stricken apathy. A coaxing note came into her light voice.

"I said it meant more to daddy to beat Brant's father at dog shows than to win in business or politics. And I said daddy was trusting you to arrange this most important thing in the world for him, and that that ought to prove how much you amount to. I even got very dramatic, Roy, and I said our—our marriage—depended on your success in this. Of course, between ourselves, it's all terribly silly, dear, like most of daddy's fads. A dog is only a dog, and dad might as well have set his heart on your catching a June bug for him. But I took care not to tell Brant Ulrich that. I made him think everything hangs on—"

Rufus G. Belden came in, fresh from his tub and from the hands of his valet. He gave the impression of a well groomed circus elephant. At sight of Roy still in a lounge suit the great man frowned. He was a stickler for promptitude at meals—which was as well, for Phyllis, left to herself, seldom would have troubled to care if dinner were on time or an hour late.

Belden's fat lips flew wide in sizzling rebuke at his secretary's tardiness in dressing. But before the first three turgid words could find utterance, Garth was guilty of another offense—namely, of interrupting his employer in an oration.

"Mr. Belden," he said, his incisive voice cutting sharply and distinctly through the looser volume of reproof, "I have blabbed about the trip to Thross. Word of it has gotten to the Ulrichs. Brant Ulrich is going over to try to get Stirling, ahead of us. It doesn't matter to whom I blabbed. I am at fault, and nobody else is. That's all."

For an instant Rufus G. Belden stared with mouth agape at his secretary. Then the fat man's face merged from pink to mauve and from mauve to blackish purple. Veins stood out on his low forehead. He clenched his ham-fists and took a step forward.

"Roy is trying to talk like a story-book hero, daddy," interposed Phyllis, moving lazily between the two men. "It was I he told. He didn't tell anyone else. He had a right to tell me, because we're more or less engaged, you know. I told Brant Ulrich."

A torrent of incoherent words burst from the big man's lips. Phyllis sighed impatiently.

"I've told you so *many* times," she said in plaintive disgust, "how utterly ridiculous you look when you get into one of your bellowing rages. Please be sane, won't you, daddy?"

As usual, her careless insolence was like a dash of ice water on her sire's boiling temper. Belden scowled mutely. Then, little by little, his face lost its purple tinge and its foolish rage, becoming once more inscrutable and shrewd. He turned to Garth.

"Phyll is right," he said with incredible mildness. "Nothing's to gain by crying over spilled milk or spilled secrets. All we can do is to gather up what's left of them. You were a fool to blab to a fluff-brained imbecile of a girl, and she was worse than a fool to blab to a swine like Brant Ulrich. But it's done."

"I—"

"Start east, tonight," commanded Belden. "Take the eleven-forty. That'll let you catch the *Roumanic*— Wasn't that the boat we wired about and that hadn't any berths left? If your train's on time you'll catch it, with two hours to spare. It will land you in England two days ahead of the boat you were going to take. I'll telegraph Symonds, in New York. He can get you aboard, even if you have to bunk in a lifeboat. Speed is the thing now. It's our one card. You can think of being comfortable afterward. . . . Hold back dinner for ten minutes," he added, slinging the command over his shoulder to the butler in the doorway. "Mr. Garth can be dressed in that time if he hustles. And that's not a patch on the hustling he is due for in the next month or two."

Garth was staring, amazed, at Belden, utterly dumfounded by the man's strange shift of manner. Phyllis was staring at Belden, too, but in less wonder than apprehension. She knew her father's moods and what lay back of them, as no mere outsider could hope to. She would have been happier if Rufus G. had been less urbane.

Decorously the butler withdrew. After repeating to the second man the decree for postponing dinner and leaving him to transmit it to the kitchen, the butler went to the telephone in his own quarters and called up the Midwestburg Athletic Club. Two minutes later he was saying in a guardedly low voice:

"Is that Mr. Brant Ulrich? This is Brunson. Mr. Garth is not going to wait till Thursday. He is leaving on the eleven-forty tonight. He is going to catch the *Roumanic*. . . . Yes, I know, sir, but Mr. Belden is going to arrange to get him aboard. . . . Yes, sir. That's why I called you up. It will have to be done on his way to the train if it's to be done at all. I—I hope, sir, you'll remember you promised it won't do any more than just lay him up for a few weeks. I'd—I'd not like to be mixed up in anything worse, even when I'm paid so generous. . . . Good night, sir."

Dinner was a lively meal. Keyed up to instant action, Roy's spirits were jubilant. Rufus G., too, not only unbent to an astonishing degree, but essayed light witticisms which though elephantine, were an indication of his change of mood.

The truck was ordered for nine o'clock to take Garth's luggage to the station, where the baggage-master received telephonic instruction to see it piled aboard at the proper time. A lower berth was reserved, also by telephone. When the last work was finished on his packing, Roy had nothing to do except to remain with Phyllis until a taxi should arrive at a little after eleven to bear him to his train.

Rufus G.—either through pity or from a rudimentary idea of sportsmanship—locked himself in his study and left the lovers to their own and each other's devices.

It was the quietest evening that Roy and the girl had spent together. Now that the moment of parting was so near, an odd silence gripped them both—a silence the greater for their cheerily persistent efforts to keep conversation from lagging. They talked fitfully, but ever there were long and longer lapses into a wordlessness that merged presently into despondency.

Roy's first gayety had departed. There were a hundred intimate and precious things he wanted to say to this adorable girl from whom he was parting for so long. There were a million things he yearned to hear her say. He craved to take into exile with him some sublimely sweet memory of her. He longed to say something which she should cherish in his absence and which should help to bridge the vast distance that was to separate them.

But, try as he would, he could speak only trivialities, or at most love words that carried scant conviction. Ever between him and her seemed to rise the unwelcome memory of her flippant tossing away of the secret he had intrusted to her. He was angry at himself for not being able to put from his mind her careless betrayal. But ever it kept crawling back as fast as he banished it.

Phyllis was at her best in lighter moods. Faced by a parting such as this, she waxed banal and all but insincere in her brave efforts to enact the required role.

Hitherto their stolen hours together had flashed by with maddening swiftness. Tonight the minutes clumped along on legs of lead. Roy found himself looking furtively at the tiny piano clock. While he was cursing himself for such treason to love he saw Phyllis's gaze stray in the same direction.

Then she drew out her vanity case and, with the absorbed air of a kitten washing its face, she dabbed make up on her faultlessly made-up face.

At last Rufus G. Belden came bustling in with the air of a man who sees off to school some child whose vacation has been a trial to the whole household.

"Brunson says the taxi is at the door, my boy," he remarked. "Haven't forgotten anything, have you? Got the checks all safe? Got the letter from Mackellar to that innkeeper cousin of his at Thross? Got the cable code clear in your mind? Good! Remember to keep me posted—as soon as you've got anything definite to post me with. Now, then, you'll have to call for your ticket and your berth at the station, and make sure about your luggage getting aboard, so you'd better go. It wouldn't do to miss the train. There isn't another till morning, you know. That would hit New York too late to connect with the *Roumanic*. It'll be touch-and-go as it is. Well, good-by. Good luck."

Tactfully he stamped out of the room ahead of them, giving Roy time to turn with outstretched arms to Phyllis. The girl ran to his clasp for a last embrace. But through her eager tenderness he seemed to read again something that was lacking, even as his own adoring farewell had in it a hint of perfunctoriness.

Puzzled and angered, Garth snatched up a small handbag and his hat and greatcoat from the hallway and hurried with Belden to the outer door. There he shook hands again with his employer and ran down the wet steps, followed by Belden's booming good-bys.

The night was thick-misted and chill. The taxi was cold and smelly and it was far from comfortable. It was a rattletrap old conveyance. Vaguely Garth wondered which of the several taxi companies was responsible for such a wretched vehicle. He looked for the card above the folded front seats. There was none. Nor, as a second glance told him, was there a meter at the right of the driver's seat. Assuredly the butler must have engaged for him some unauthorized "wildcat" cab.

Then the jolting grew more violent. The taxi was making its way at high speed down a rutted hill. The road to the station from Beldencroft was of smoothest asphalt. The driver appeared to be trying a short cut. Then Garth reflected there was no shorter route to the station than by the asphalt highway. Indeed, that was the only direct means of getting to the depot.

He leaned forward and pounded on the glass in front

of him. The driver's only form of recognition of the hail was to step on the gas. So far as the ice-cold fog would permit Roy to see their whereabouts, they were descending a steep hill, between tree trunks.

There was but one such hill road anywhere near Beldencroft—a precipitous byway which led through lonely woods, toward the open country in the direction farthest from the station.

In exasperation at the driver's stupidity, Roy flung open the door and shouted:

"You're on the wrong road!"

By way of reply the cab came to a jarring standstill at the most desolate spot on the whole lonely hillside. For a moment its bleary lights illumined four fog-shaddowed human figures that stood, as if waiting, about twenty feet from the cab. One of the four loomed gigantic in the mist. At the road edge to the left were propped two black motorcycles, each with a side car.

This much and only this much did Roy Garth see before the taxi's faint lights were turned abruptly off.

Then came the rush of shod feet toward the cab. Through the mist, beside the doorway through which Roy was leaning out, bulked a huge and dimly discerned body. The far door of the cab was wrenched wide. From either side, unseen men flung themselves upon the passenger.

Something—perhaps a blackjack, perhaps a bar of iron—grazed Roy's head, and smashed to tinkling flinders the glass front. Hands were clawing and gripping at him in the murk. A second blow from another invisible weapon smote him glancingly on the shoulder, numbing his arm, then spent its chief force in splintering a door-frame.

If Garth could not see his assailants, neither could they see him. Fighter's instinct told him this, as the noise of breaking glass and rending wood roused him from his first amazement at the silent preconcerted attack.

His handbag between his knees, he slumped quickly to the bottom of the car; at the same time writhing eel-like out of his greatcoat.

Heavy and thick and loose was the ulster. Thus, by dint of speed and adroitness, Garth was able to rip free from it, while the invisible hands still clutched at its collar and shoulders and groped to pinion his arms.

In practically the same lightning gesture, he seized his heavy little handbag and dived head-foremost out of the car doorway. As he sprang, he swung the bag. The missile found its mark in some thudding and reeling obstacle. Garth's head butted with terrific force into the meridian of the giant who was tossing aside the empty greatcoat he had seized.

There was a gasp, a doubling of a mighty body, an involuntary cry from someone else. Then, for the merest atom of time, Garth was free. He had found his footing as easily as a tossed cat. Hatless, ulsterless, gripping his bag as his one available weapon, he sprang backward, turning and running.

At once the whole baffled pack were after him.

Hampered as the assailants were by thick darkness, there was time for Garth to have plunged into the road-side woods and, running silently, to elude them. But that was not his plan. In the midst of his fury and peril he had sense to understand the situation.

He knew these four men had not been waiting in so desolate a spot on the bare chance of waylaying and robbing a possible passer-by. He knew the driver had not missed the main road and brought him to this out-of-the-way place by accident. Moreover, in the single fleeting glimpse of the four, through the fog, he had recognized past all reasonable doubt the wide shoulders and oddly animal head-carriage of the giant who led the assault.

This had given Garth his clue to the whole scene and had awakened in him a fierce resolve to lose his life, if need be, sooner than let Ulrich succeed in the ruse to make him miss his all-important train.

As on more than one desperate football field, Roy had laid out his own plan of action before even he slid free of his cumbering greatcoat.

Failure of his plan meant weeks in hospital at the very best, if not death or permanent maiming. But to run into the safety of the woods meant the missing of the only train which could enable him to catch the *Roumanic*. He had but one chance, and that a ridiculously slight one. Yet that chance he was stubbornly set on taking.

Wherefore, in his instant of freedom, before the others could charge him, Garth fled on soundless feet toward the two motorcyles. His wide out-flung arms missed them. But he stumbled head-first over the nearer of the two. Without stopping to recover his balance he shoved the machine ahead of him into the road, then started its luckily warm engine with a stamp of his foot.

The burring racket guided the blundering quartet at once to him. On they rushed. Garth swung the stout bag about him in a swishing blind circle.

The bag found a mark. Roy did not know what part of what man it collided with. But he heard a noisy tumble in the road mud. Then he kicked with deadly intensity at someone who was tackling him low.

The cycle's engine sang and roared into full life. Almost upsetting it, as he ran into someone who dashed at him from in front, Garth was under way.

"Lights!" roared Brant Ulrich's voice.

There was a flare from behind that made blindingly brilliant the rutted road. A pistol shot flicked the elbow of Roy's coat. Another slapped the machine, sideways, making it careen dangerously.

Meanwhile the second motorcycle was purring and coughing. Now it was in motion.

Down the precipitous stony slope lurched the two cycles at a dizzily drunken pace.

A wild exhilaration swept through Garth. True, he was not headed for the station. But his knowledge of the region told him that any one of three successive intersecting roads, from a mile to two miles farther on, would take him thither.

Then a sick dread killed his exultation.

Not a week earlier he had traversed this hillside by-way, in one of his long walks, meaning to return, by a path lower down, to Beldencroft. But he had had to go back the way he came. This because a prematurely early freshet had torn away the jerry-built bridge at the bottom of the sharp incline. The bridge had spanned a thirty-foot drop into a rock-sided creek.

Downhill, straight toward this unbridged chasm, his motorcycle was whirling him at something like eighty miles an hour. Close behind thundered the second machine, scarce fifty feet to his rear.

CHAPTER FOUR

IN A CHEERLESSLY barren little room under whose low slant roof one half-sized window was tucked sat Roy Garth, writing. He was finishing a long letter to his employer. The first sheet of his letter, lying on the crazy deal table beside him, was headed, "Thross, Inverness-shire, Scotland, March 11."

For a moment Roy looked up from his tediously long epistle. His gaze strayed through the open window out over the moorland that hemmed in the straggling little Highland village.

Billowing sweeps of bare hill stretched away to the misty horizon in the early morning sunshine, slopes smeared with dry heather so black that a fire seemed to have scourged the hills. In another few months these miles of heather would be purple and white and would give forth a tingling aroma in the summer sun. The gorse, too, and the bracken, would be in riot of bloom.

But today a scatter of golden-yellow broom and hedge-side patches of primrose and a stray violet or two alone foretold the season of blossom.

In a field a half mile away a blue-shirted farmer was

plowing the dark earth, guiding two big red horses. In his wake trailed a thousand black-headed white gulls, hopping eagerly after the plow and snatching insects from the turned up furrow.

The snowy horde of gulls was accompanied by scores of solemnly lofty English pheasants and long-billed gray oyster-catchers and crested plover, all chasing fearlessly up to the very tail of the plow, like a motley brood of chickens at feeding time.

Far along an upland trail a squat shepherd was convoying a herd of grayish sheep, black of face and with wool as long and as straight as a Shetland pony's forelock. An undersized black collie kept the jostling mass of sheep in steady progress and clean formation.

A brawling rivulet cut a flashing course through its tangled braes to the distant fire-blue loch. Beyond the loch shone lofty snow-clad peaks, rank on rank. Rooks cawed and scolded in a copse of stiff yew trees in a sunny old churchyard.

Nearer, the mean village of stone cots huddled around the four sides of a steep and craggy hillock. The hill was crowned by a plateau whereon stood a dilapidated gray castle of untold age and general air of disreputableness.

Long did Roy Garth's gaze rest on this high cluster of ancient stone with its tumble-down outer wall and its one squat crenelated turret. Then he bent again to the task of writing his letter to Rufus G. Belden.

Well [*resumed the epistle*], *there they were, after me, all of them. I don't know if there were one or two on the other motorcycle. But those who weren't on it kept firing pot shots down the hill at me. Then I remembered the bridge at the foot was gone. I was going too fast to stop, with such a muddy and steep road under me and with the other cycle just behind. So I set my teeth and kept on.*

Just as I got to the edge of the creek, my light showed me some one had put a single wide board across it, to serve as a footway till the bridge could be repaired. There was only one thing for me to do, and I did it. There was no stopping. So I steered for that plank, and I prayed it might be wide enough for me to ride over and not weak enough to buckle under me.

I hit it at about seventy-five miles an hour. It wabbled and jounced as I spun across it. I got to the other side. (That is why I'm writing to you from Thross and not from a hospital.) The cycle behind me must have skidded, or else I was between its driver and the plank and he couldn't see it. I suppose he thought the bridge was still there, because, as I whizzed on, I heard a crash and a yell. He had gone in.

It wasn't Ulrich's voice that yelled, so I infer he wasn't aboard. I cut through the next crossroad, and got to the station as the train was stopping. It was an hour late at New York, so I had to jump for the boat. I caught it by only a handful of spare seconds.

Remember I can't swear that it was Brant Ulrich who framed the hold-up and who was the leader of it.

I couldn't see him distinctly enough to take oath to him. But I am morally sure I recognized him and recognized his voice, too. Besides, nobody else would have had any object in putting me out of business.

Better give Brunson a call-down for not being more careful about the kind of taxi he orders from town. I don't see how he could have gotten hold of such a rig. The driver was in Ulrich's pay, of course; but how did he happen to induce Brunson to hire him to drive me to the station? That's what I can't understand.

As I said, I got here to Thross. It's a God-forsaken hamlet, seven miles from Ferrol, the nearest town with a railroad station. I gave Jamie Mackellar's letter of introduction to his cousin who runs this atrocious inn, and here I'm staying. Ian Mackellar (the innkeeper) is a dour old cuss who talks as if each of his words was his last shilling. I haven't been able to get much out of him in the way of information, except that the Macbeath never allows tourists inside his castle (I'm a rich American tourist, you'll recall, traveling up here to get over a nervous collapse), and that he won't speak to a foreigner if he can help it.

He's a bachelor—Macbeath, not Ian Mackellar—and his niece, a Miss Kathleen Macbeath, keeps house for him. I saw her, today, from a distance. She is tall and wholesome-looking and walks like an athlete. I saw her on the way to Loch Thross.

Yes, and I saw something lots more interesting. I saw Stirling. The collie was with Miss Macbeath. I hear they go on long walks together every day. (I don't blame her. It must be deadly slow for her, up at that tumble-down castle, with only her grouchy uncle and the servants.) Stirling was too far away for me to study him closely. But, from the glimpse I got of him, he is all Jamie said.

I'm not going to bother you with any more letters until I have something definite. I just wanted you to know I'm here and that I realize Brant Ulrich will be over at any time, now; and that I haven't many days to waste.

He enveloped and sealed the letter, then scribbled a line to Phyllis.

He was bewildered at his own difficulty in writing to the girl of his heart. He had been sending her a letter at every possible opportunity since he left America, ten days earlier. And each had been harder to write, for some reason, than its predecessor.

But at last his perfunctory labor was ended and he went down to the inn taproom to drop his two letters into the post bag.

He had risen early to write, as the one mail a day was taken across to the seven-mile-distant railroad town of Ferrol, at nine in the morning. The local postman—a small and fox-faced oldster with a visored cap—carried it on foot and then returned in like manner to Thross with the day's local post bag from the Ferrol railroad station.

Youth and health made Garth eat a stupendous breakfast in the shabby inn parlor, but he was far from feeling as jauntily at ease as he had tried to appear in his letter to Phyllis Belden.

Now that he was on the ground he was confronted by an *impasse*. True, he had had the luck and the wit to elude Ulrich and get to Thross some days earlier than his rival could hope to. But now he was here, there seemed nothing feasible to do.

True, he had sent a note to the castle, on his arrival, presenting his respects to the Laird and describing himself as a health-seeking American traveler who was anxious to see the interior of the historic castle of King Macbeth.

If only he could get inside the walls and establish acquaintanceship with their owner, he felt he might be able to bring Macbeath to listen to reason as to selling the collie; the more so since every inch of castle and of village bespoke the chief's poverty.

An hour later, the boy by whom he had sent the tactful request came back to him with his own note. Athwart the bottom of the page was written in a tiny cramped hand:

The Macbeath presents his compliments, such as they are, to Mr. Roy Garth of America, and begs to inform him that the Macbeath does not like foreigners; nor, for that matter, does he like the average non-foreigner. Therefore the Macbeath must forego the very limited rapture of receiving Mr. Roy Garth at his unworthy ancestral home.

Moreover, you poor ignoramus, even a guide-book-lapping Yankee ought to know this is not the "historic castle of King Macbeth." It was not built until nearly three centuries later. The original castle of King Macbeth was probably made of mud and wattle. If you wish to see a sweet and conventionally romantic-looking castle, I suggest that you drive over to Cawdor, a few miles from here. It is a show place. My poor home is not. I suggest also—and with much more fervor—that you refrain from annoying me by further futile requests.

The boorish refusal roused Garth's fighting blood, as had the attack upon him on the steep hillside road near Beldencroft. Anew, he vowed he would get inside the castle, by hook or by crook or by force, and would lay his mission in diplomatic form before the Macbeath.

All night Roy had lain awake, racking his brains. At dawn an idea had flitted through his bemused mind—an idea so fantastic that he laughed it away. But it would not stay away. Unconsciously he found himself elaborating on it as he ate his breakfast.

His table was close to the inn parlor's window, which overlooked the scraggly high street and the tiny patch of village square. It was the region's weekly market day. Already the square was beginning to fill with small farmers and the like, some with vegetables, some driving long-haired and black-faced sheep. One was piloting a dozen shaggy auburn Highland steers; small, rough animals with a spread of horn quite out of proportion to their squat size, and with manelike forelocks.

Idly Garth watched the gathering marketers. The hour was early, yet the thrifty buyers and sellers were flocking fast to the barter. Hidden behind the muslin window curtain that shook in the morning breeze, Roy looked out on the Old World spectacle in the square before him.

"Will this fine weather hold, do you think?" he asked a gnarled carter who loitered past the window.

"Aiblins aye. Aiblins na. Aiblins eh-heh."

Having safeguarded his glum reply from argument on all sides, he stumped on.

From out the inn taproom strode a stout young man in full panoply of kilt and tartan and sporran. From one sock peeped a silver dagger hilt. In his bonnet he sported three short eagle feathers. Apparently he was a well-to-do drover. He seemed to have drunk more for breakfast than he had eaten, for he was merry and swaggering in his salutations to fellow-drovers.

Though the tartan and kilt are seldom worn nowadays, except as holiday garb, yet the stout young man was arrayed as if for a Highland festival. His companions grinned as they noted his costume. But their grins were covert. By the semi-respect wherewith they treated him, he was a person of some local consequence.

As he came out into the street, another oddly apparelled figure approached him from the side of the square nearest the road that led down from the castle rock. The second man was tall and meager of form and was dressed in what at first seemed a brand-new and fashionably cut black suit of some forty years ago; with an Inverness cape dragging from one shoulder. His hat was a glossy beaver. In his hand he carried a gold-headed staff on which he leaned somewhat heavily.

A closer glance showed that the suit was threadbare and plenteously darned. The hat's nap was worn away. The Hessian boots were patched. The flowing black cloak showed longer wear than did the ancient coat beneath it.

But these were minor details to Garth as he caught sight of the tall man's face. Grizzled hair framed a lean and bone-white countenance, clean shaven, and with searing lines crisscrossing it like Heidelberg dueling scars. Black bushy brows slashed the curiously white visage. They slanted upward and sidewise, Mephistoph-eles-wise, above snakelike black eyes that smoldered as with banked fires.

The crowd made way eagerly for the gaunt new-comer. Hats and caps and bonnets were doffed as he passed. He paid no slightest heed to the timidly reverential greetings of those he stalked past, but made his way directly toward the gaily tartaned Highland drover. The two met just beneath the open window from behind whose curtain Roy Garth was surveying them.

The drover doffed his bonnet with jaunty respect, then replaced it on his crop-haired head. The old man paid no more heed to the salute than he had paid to the cap-touchings of the lesser marketers. He walked up close to the drover, whose jauntiness wilted visibly beneath the searing glare of the black eyes flashing out at him from under those black brows.

The old man's glower focused on the three short eagle feathers which adorned the drover's bonnet. The thin old lips parted in a rasped question:

"Sennach, do you know what the three eagle feathers stand for? Do you?"

He spoke as though rebuking a stray dog. The drover winced, grinned uncomfortably, fidgeted, and made as if to answer. But before he could frame his halting reply the rasping voice continued:

"One eagle feather is the symbol of a Scottish gentleman. Two eagle feathers are the insignia of a chieftain. Three eagle feathers are the insignia of a *chief!* Every weanling bairn north of Aberfeldy knows that."

He paused, to let the lesson sink in. Sennach grinned afresh, but more feebly, and he turned crimson as the crowd gathered to watch the scene. Twice he essayed to speak. Twice, under the ice-hard glint of those ancient black eyes, his words died unborn.

Out shot the gaunt man's clawlike right hand. The talon fingers gripped one of the eagle feathers, ripping it from the bonnet and tossing it into the dirt.

"You are not a chief!" he rasped.

A second time the withered hand shot forth, and a second eagle feather fell into the muck.

"You are not a chieftain!" admonished the harsh voice.

Sennach cringed back against the wall, but made no move to resent or check the affront. A third time the bony fingers clutched an eagle plume and flicked it to the ground.

"You are not a gentleman!" snarled the old man.

Someone in the crowd sniggered. The oldster shot a glance of reproof at him, and the snigger ceased. Turning back to the embarrassed and cowed drover, the gaunt stranger resumed:

"You are wearing a Sutherland war tartan. You have no claim to it. But that is the Sutherland clansmen's affair, not mine. The Sutherland motto is, *'Touch Not the Cat but with a Glove.'* I'll improve on it for you: *'Touch Not the Cur but with a Boot!'* "

With agility surprising in one so old, he spun the flabbergasted drover around and planted a kick in the most salient part of Sennach's plump anatomy. Then, without another word or look for his victim, he strolled on his way, disappearing in the reverential crowd.

An inn serving-maid had come to remove the remains of Garth's breakfast and had remained to watch over the guest's shoulder the encounter between the drover and his persecutor. Now, making certain the man in black had passed out of hearing, she laughed shrilly at Sennach's pitiful discomfiture. Roy turned to her in eager curiosity.

"Who was that old chap?" he asked. "And do people hereabouts let themselves be kicked like that? Don't they stand up for themselves, at all?"

Instantly the maid's giggles were checked. She made cold reply:

"The Laird may e'en do as he sees fit to do, and wha

will gainsay him? That will 'a been the Macbeath, sir, what done the kicking out yon, the noo. If you or another had kicked Wullie Sennach, Wullie wad ha' thrashed you fine, gin he was brawny enow. Gin he wasna' brawny enow, ye'd have found yersel' with the blade of his *sgian dhu* amang your rib-bones."

She departed with her tray of greasy dishes. Garth stared far out in vain hope of catching another glimpse of the redoubtable Macbeath—the chief who in this enlightened twentieth century could kick in public a free man and pass on unmolested. Mightily the young American wondered. For the first time he could believe Jamie Mackellar's tales of the humble reverence in which the wilder Highlanders still hold their hereditary lairds.

Then, adown the winding stony road from the castle came a girl and a dog, moving toward the byway which skirted the little market place, in the direction of distant Loch Thross.

At once Garth was on his feet. The brief sight of these two had brought back to his memory the fantastic plan he had brooded on overnight. In his momentary excitement it seemed no longer fantastic, but gaily adventurous.

He caught up his cap and bolted out of the inn by a rear door, half walking, half running, across the rough ground, in a short cut toward the loch. He had a start on the girl and her dog. Moreover, they were traveling by the winding hill road, while he was striking straight across country.

Not giving himself time to consider Garth hastened over the rock-scattered moor, up the sharp slope, and toward the clump of boulders which jutted far out into the cold waters of the mountain loch.

Kathleen Macbeath had set out, as usual, for her brisk morning walk around the loch, with the golden young collie, Stirling, dancing delightedly about her. But instead of going straight to the loch path, she detoured in a way to pass through the market square of Thross and by the meager inn.

The day before, she had heard her uncle cursing luridly at the impudence of an American globe-trotter who had found his way far off the tourist routes to Thross, and who, forsooth, had the effrontery to ask leave to bring himself and probably his objectionable guidebook to the sacred precincts of the castle itself, in the idiotic hope of beholding the place where the first Macbeth and his wife had murdered King Duncan.

Kathleen had been keenly interested in the news. Immured in the lonely ruin atop the rocky hill, day after day, year after year, with no greater excitement than her walks with Stirling or a very rare visit of state to the Macbeath from some other down-at-heel laird, or a market day, or a Spring Holiday Fair, a new face in the neighborhood was theme for genuine interest.

Since the day when she had left the prim and primitive "finishing school," outside of Perth, two years earlier, at her mother's death, and had come hither as housekeeper and chatelaine to her long-dead father's eldest brother, she had seen almost nobody from the great outer world and had been thrown wholly on herself for entertainment.

The Macbeath was genuinely fond of her, in his own crabbedly sardonic way. But he let her do pretty much as she might please, so long as she managed his servants and looked after his castle and kept expenses down. This last task was no sinecure. The Laird was increasingly poor, and credit was increasingly difficult to find, even in the loyal region where he lorded it.

Bills and duns and threatened lawsuits and the difficulty of meeting mortgage payments—these were the chief topics of discourse at the castle nowadays. The Macbeath was in cruelly sore straits at every hand. Nor did his ever-pressing poverty improve his saturnine temper. True, he did not wreak this temper on Kathleen herself. But she alone was exempt from its scorpion lashes, and the sufferings of servants and humble clansmen under it were a constant sorrow to her.

Today her tour through the market square was unavailing, so far as concerned getting a glimpse of the American visitor. On all sides bonnets and other headgear were touched civilly as the Laird's heiress made her way along the square. But each and every face and each and every name was wearisomely familiar to her. Ian Mackellar stood in the doorway of his inn, chatting with a shepherd. Shepherd and innkeeper touched their forelocks to Kathleen as she came by. She paused, and said to Mackellar in elaborate unconcern:

"I hear you have a new guest. An American, isn't he?"

"Yes, miss," returned the innkeeper. "A main queer one, too, I'm thinking. We'll just have been speirin' about him, Tobis here and me. The furriner be tired in the nerves, he says, and he's resting here a bit. But he just shot out of back door the noo, and across Horrock Muir, like he was rode by the witches. Run, he did, more'n walk. Straight for the loch. What's to send any man there in such a pother of hurry I'll ask ye, miss? Queer he is. Like all they American multimillionaire folk."

The girl nodded, and went onward. The stranger had gone toward the loch? Well, she was on her way thither, anyhow. So perhaps she might chance to see him, after all. Not that it mattered in the least, she told herself.

Stirling, the big young collie, had stopped to sniff in lofty friendliness at a black little sheep-herding collie that jogged past in the wake of a straggly line of black-faced Highland sheep and a scattering of gawky baby lambs. Now he raced forward again, catching up with Kathleen and thrusting a friendly cold nose into her idly swinging hand.

Together, girl and dog breasted the hill slope of the heather-strewn moor, toward the loch. They passed by the noisily chuckling sample-size waterfall which cascaded foaming into a brook; then they neared the rocky edge of the loch itself.

A turn of the path, as they toiled upward, revealed to them a stocky man in tweeds standing at the brink of a shelf of piled rocks that protruded out into the lake. He was standing there idly, looking down into the clear deeps of the water. He did not appear to note their approach, so interestedly was he peering into the loch.

Kathleen's path would bring her many yards to south of him. She was well pleased that this should be. She had no desire to meet the stranger face to face, but merely to satisfy her mild curiosity about him at a distance, as now she was doing.

Her casual glance at the American afforded her no special pleasure. He was not a strikingly romantic figure, with his powerfully stocky body and curly reddish hair and tiptilted nose and square jaw. True, the innkeeper had said Garth was a multimillionaire. But then most Americans were supposed to be multimillionaires, weren't they? Vast wealth, in this case, did not imply physical beauty.

The girl was moving off to southward, away from the lone figure on the rock. As she went she smiled at the thought that so rich a man should be forced to stop at the miserable inn of Thross. It must assuredly seem to him a fearsome privation, after his own marble palaces and yachts and cars and his army of trained servants.

The collie had dropped behind, to investigate a deserted fox-earth on the brackened hillside. Now with fast-pattering steps Stirling came bounding up the slope to his mistress. As he came he caught scent and sight of the man who stood on the narrow jut of rock beyond.

Stirling halted, growling a throaty inquiring challenge

to the intruder. The man spun about at sound of the growl.

The sudden turn made him lose his footing on the slippery bit of rock-jut. He strove in vain to regain his balance. Then with a loud exclamation of impatience he lurched sidewise and tumbled over the ledge.

His powerful body smote the water with a resounding splash.

CHAPTER FIVE

KATHLEEN paused in her walk, to watch the accident. Much ado had she not to laugh at thought of the damage the icy loch water would wreak on the well-cut tweed outing suit, and its dampening and chilling effect on the nerve-wrecked foreigner. Stirling, too, was hugely interested in the spectacle. Trotting to the rock-jut, he stood with head on one side and tulip-ears cocked, while he blinked amusedly down at the widening circle of water under which Roy had sunk.

But almost at once Kathleen's incipient laughter changed to vague worry. According to all precedent, the man's curly reddish hair should have appeared instantly above the surface and his stocky body should have struck out for shore. But he did not appear.

The girl wondered if the rock formation could extend outward under water and if he might have been stunned by striking his head against a submerged boulder. If so—

She ran at top speed to the rock-jut and stood there beside Stirling, just as there was a new rippling of the disturbed water.

The man was rising to the surface—not gasping and sputtering and swimming, but slowly and without voluntary motion. His back and his shoulders emerged slowly, inertly, his head still invisible.

Thus for a moment he lay. Then even more slowly he began to sink again.

It was a really creditable performance. Roy had not enacted it since he was a boy. In those early days he had acquired pleasing proficiency in the gruesome old aquatic stunt of "drowned man."

With a convulsive jerk, now, he appeared to come partly to his senses, for he struggled feebly. The struggle brought his blankly expressionless face above water for an instant—a maneuver made strongly advisable by his need for a deep gulp of air. Then, still moving feebly and awkwardly, he began again to sink.

To all appearances not only was he half stunned, but he had not even the most rudimentary knowledge of swimming. Also there was a smudge of blood on his forehead. He was settling slowly into the blue depths, despite his faint attempts to keep afloat.

Girl and dog awoke to a realization of the peril at the same time. With a sharp bark Stirling launched himself in air and plunged into the lake, swimming strongly in circles, his head and shoulders high, as he ranged in search of the vanished man.

Kathleen wasted no more time than did the dog. Diving clean and straight, her slenderly athletic body clove the water. Down she went, as true as a flung spear, her outreached hands groping for the weakly striving Garth.

Her fingers closed about the shoulders of his coat. With all her supple young strength she fought her way to the surface, dragging Roy upward with her. As man and girl reappeared, Stirling set his strong teeth in Garth's tweed shoulder and churned the water in his attempt to tow the victim shoreward.

Kathleen swam easily alongside, one hand holding Garth's face above the ripples, while she reinforced the collie's straining efforts to tow the heavy body to land.

Athletes at the Midwestburg Athletic Club, where twice Roy had won cups for distance and sprint swimming, would have gaped in amaze at his present helplessness.

On shipboard, Garth had chanced upon a library volume of French comedies, among the list *Le Voyage de M. Perrichon*. The whimsical plot of the farce had stuck in his mind. It told of a rich old simpleton whose daughter was loved by two men. One of the two saved Perrichon's life. Presently the old fellow grew to hate the youth to whom he owed such a tremendous service.

The second suitor, with rare knowledge of human nature, had pretended to be in mortal danger and had arranged that Perrichon should seem to save his life. Instantly Perrichon had become his devoted friend and admirer and had given him his daughter's hand in marriage—living up to the oft-proven theory that we care far more for those we help than for those who help us.

It was this cynical tale which had given Roy his plan.

Outside a dime novel the hero seldom has a chance to save the life of the heroine or indeed the life of anyone who may be of service to him.

It was not likely that Garth could place the Macbeath or Kathleen under obligations to himself and thus win their acquaintanceship. But he saw no reason why he could not take a leaf from the French play's moral and win favor by placing himself under deep obligation to Kathleen or to the Laird. Hence his spectacular semblance of drowning.

As a matter of fact, his forehead had come into sharp grazing contact with a stone's corner, far under water. This, while wholly unintended, was realistic testimony to his mishap's genuineness.

Girl and collie struggled gamely and strenuously at the task of bringing the half-lifeless body to shore. The distance to the nearest patch of shelving beach was only a few yards. Presently Kathleen was standing up in knee-deep water and even Stirling's waving feet found toehold amid the pebbles. The dog let go of the man's coat and stood panting, up to his own shoulders among the ripples.

Kathleen lifted Garth's supinely heavy body to a sitting posture. Roy opened his eyes and peered dazedly about him. Then he slumped again and would have been submerged had not Kathleen's strong young arms held him up.

Worriedly, the girl looked down into the sagging man's face. She had read that the almost-drowned are of an unnatural bluish-purple complexion. Now she branded the statement as another of the countless accepted literary falsehoods. This man's face was ruddily bronzed, though his eyes were shut and his well-shaped head rolled limp.

The morning breeze blew shrewdly about her own wet body, whipping her drenched walking skirt and chilling the cascades of water that showered down from her loosened masses of brown hair. She set her white little teeth and bent to the herculean effort of lifting or dragging the man's hundred-and-seventy-five inert pounds of weight to the bank.

But with a spasmodic start Roy came to himself again and lurched blunderingly to his feet. Floundering, swaying, all but collapsing, supported by the girl's arms, he staggered to shore. There he collapsed again, at full length, among the lochside bracken.

Skillfully Kathleen toiled over him, moving his arms up and down to restore his breathing powers and to start in motion his supposedly retarded heart. In a few seconds Garth opened his eyes, looking up at her in sleepy bewilderment.

He saw above him a flushed face, straight of brow, level of gaze, brown-eyed, steady of mouth and jaw. Not a beautiful or seductive face, perhaps; assuredly with none of Phyllis Belden's willful daintiness; but wholesome and unafraid, and with a certain elusive winsomeness in the depths of the eyes and in the dimpled corners of the firm little mouth.

A queer twinge of shame ran through Roy as he looked into the eyes so close above his own.

Up to now he had been congratulating himself smugly on the cleverness of his acting and on his ruse's prospects of success. He owed nothing to this Highland girl and her grim uncle. He was planning them no ill. All he desired was a chance to pay an outrageously high sum for a dog—a price which would go far toward lifting them out of the poverty that was theirs. To do this, apparently, he must make the acquaintance of the castle folk.

His letter of request had been flouted. Thus he was seeking the only way he could think of to obtain admission to the castle and a chance to meet its master on equal terms. He had chosen a method which had entailed a ducking for himself in icy waters and a bad crack on the head. There seemed no reason for his momentary sting of shame.

Kathleen Macbeath's flush deepened as she saw and misread the look in his eyes. Now that his face was visible, he was better-looking than she had thought. She liked his level eyes and the collie-like glint of hidden mischief lurking behind them. Also, in his weakness, he seemed so helpless, so dependent on her, in spite of his size and his appearance of mighty strength.

There was a throb of maternal protectiveness in her heart for the stricken youth whom she had saved from sudden death. In an oddly illogical way she was aware of a feeling of responsibility for him, now that she had snatched him back to life.

The innkeeper had said the American was nerve-wrecked and had come to the peaceful Highlands for rest. Surely this shock of immersion in chill March waters must have been bad for him! For the matter of that, a half-sick nervous convalescent could not be very comfortable nor very happy in that bleak little inn at Thross, with its iron-hard beds and stuffy rooms and bad food.

Mingled with her strange maternal tenderness for Roy was a gush of pity as she conjectured the discomfort that must be his, here in this far land, alone and sick. Truly, the author of *Le Voyage de M. Perrichon* had a startling clear knowledge of human nature!

"I'm—I'm horribly sorry to have been such a pest!" muttered Garth, his voice strengthening as he went on. "I was silly enough to tumble overboard, wasn't I? And then, you—didn't you help me out? You and—and your dog? There doesn't—seem to be any way to thank you. But—"

"Don't try to talk," she adjured him. "Lie still till you're feeling better. Then we'll—"

"You're soaking wet!" he broke in with real remorse. "And you're shivering. I—"

"Yes," she admitted, smiling to keep her teeth from chattering. "One seldom takes a swim in Loch Thross without getting a bit dampish. But it's nothing. As soon as we get in motion we'll warm up. The sun is coming out again, too. That will help. . . . No, no! Don't try to move till you're perfectly able to."

This as he sprang unaided to his feet and stopped to

pick up and wrap about her wet shoulders the jacket she had thrown aside when she dived for him.

"I'm ashamed!" he declared, and with more truth than semblance. "Come, let's hurry back to Thross! You ought to be in dry clothes as soon as you can. Then—"

He checked his impulsive speech, not only because its tone had none of the weakness or other defects which one is prone to associate with the voice of the half drowned, but because as he jumped up he found himself confronting the red-gold collie, Stirling.

For the first time he had a clear view of the dog that was the goal of his journey. The collie's massive burnished coat was still lank from his dousing, but it had fluffed out enough by dint of vigorous shaking to give an idea of its perfection of quantity and quality.

Every classic line of the collie's frame stood out in clean relief—the great shoulders, the narrow waist, the barrel ribs and deep chest, the powerful quarters and straight limbs. The head might well have been chiseled by a sculptor. In contour and in expression it was flawless.

Garth caught his breath. Here was a super-collie well worth crossing the world to gape at. Nothing in all America had Roy seen to approach Stirling's excellence. Not even Lochinvar Bobby or any other of the stars of the dog-show firmament. With such a collie the Beldencroft kennels could cut a wide swathe of dog-show victories from coast to coast.

Gravely, if whimsically, the dog was surveying Garth;

evidently sizing up the man as keenly as Roy was sizing him. But it was into Garth's eyes alone that Stirling looked, as if seeking to read there the man's very soul. Long and earnestly he stared, head on one side.

Then, sedately, he moved forward and laid a white and wet little forepaw on the American's knee, thrusting his muzzle against Roy's hand. Stirling had read what he had sought to read, and the result evidently was up to whatever test for friendship the collie had set.

Garth bent down, taking the classically chiseled head in his two hands and shaking it gently as he talked to the dog. Kathleen forgot her own chilliness and Garth's supposed sad plight.

"Why, he has adopted you as a pal!" she exclaimed in astonishment. "Stirling has vouched for you! Except for my uncle and myself, he has never made friends with anyone, before. He is civilly aloof with people who have the sense to let him alone. If they don't, he induces them to—with his teeth. But he never made friends, like this."

"I wonder if the 'Perrichon' theory applies to dogs, too," mused Roy, to himself, as he petted the silken head which Stirling laid against his wet knee. "But that isn't why he's accepted me as a chum. I know collies too well for that. Just as I seem to be almost the only man alive who has the sense to know that dogs will make friends with a crook as willingly as they'll make friends with a saint, if they happen to like him."

Aloud he said:

"Forgive me for keeping you waiting. But you can't blame me if my breath was taken away by the sight of this glorious collie of yours. I've never seen his like. You must be tremendously proud to own him."

"I would be," she answered, "if I owned him. But I don't. He belongs to my uncle. My uncle," she broke off to explain, "is named Macbeath. I am Kathleen Macbeath. We live at the castle, in Thross. You're Mr. Garth, aren't you? I think I heard my uncle say he had a note from you, didn't I?"

Their eyes met. Through no volition of either of them, they broke into laughter. It was a long laugh, a gaily hearty laugh, a laugh that bridged days and days of otherwise formal overtures and made them all at once feel genuinely well acquainted with each other.

"Oh dear!" she exclaimed, her eyes aswim with laughter tears, "I shall never learn to be diplomatic and tactful. In the first place, I ought to have seemed not to know you ever wrote to him, when I know the horrid answer you got. Then, instead of talking very fast about something else, to cover up my blunder, I laughed and spoiled it all. I'm—"

"No," he denied, "You *un*-spoiled it all. That laugh of ours has taken away the last speck of bad taste in my mouth that his letter put there. It was abominably intrusive of me to write at all and ask to butt in on his privacy. I deserved what I got. Well, anyhow, his grand dog has accepted me as a friend. That's *something*, even if the Laird has better taste than to want an American poking all over his home and asking foolish questions about its architecture."

As he talked they had started toward Thross, stepping

fast, side by side, their long and practiced strides coinciding perfectly; the collie frisking on ahead and now and then running back to one or the other of his human friends.

"Are you getting any less frozen?" asked Garth as they slowed to a walk after running down a steep pitch of moor.

"I'm splendidly warm, now," she answered, adding, with a tinge of worry, "but *you* must be feeling worse every minute, after being under water and having your nerves so jangled by the fall and— Oh!" she broke off, in real concern, as the mass of curls on his forehead blew aside in a gust of moorland breeze and showed an ugly bruise from which a few drops of blood were oozing—"oh, you have hurt your head! How careless of me not to have made you examine it! And here I've been letting you walk ever so fast and even run! You never said a word about it, either," she finished reproachfully.

But she was aware of an admiration for the breeding of the man who had sought to save her from distress by hiding such a hurt from her. And she liked him the more for making light of it and for refusing to stop at the rillside to wash and bind the bruise.

"Ordinarily," he said, when he had forced the talk into other and less personal channels—"ordinarily I should risk a snub by asking you if I may call while I'm in Thross. But after your uncle made known his views so very frankly, I'm afraid it would hardly do for me to ask. Still, you go walking every morning, don't you? Perhaps sometime—if I'll promise very solemnly not to fall into any lochs or bump my thick head against a rock—you'll let me go along?"

He spoke almost timidly, yet with a boyish eagerness which awoke again in her that first throb of maternal solicitude toward him.

"How did you know I go walking every morning?" she asked in surprise.

"Because the first sight I saw, the morning I got here, was you and your great dog starting down the road from the castle. Then again the next morning and—"

"I didn't know we had an audience. How lonely you must be when all you can do to amuse yourself is to look out of an inn window all day! And you haven't been well, either," she went on, the motherliness now creeping more noticeably into her pleasant Scotch voice. "What miserable memories of Thross you'll be carrying away with you! I'm so sorry!"

Again he fought back a feeling of shame, as if at the cheating of some trustful child. To hide the unbidden twinge he replied loudly and volubly:

"I shall carry away no memories of Thross at all, just yet. I'm planning to stay here for a month or so longer, at the very least. They say Maytime in the Highlands is something to remember forever. . . . For your sake, I could wish I had come here a month or two earlier, while the loch was still frozen. Then I could have spared you the ducking you got today. At worst, you and your dog would only have had to drag me across the ice, instead of diving for me."

"You would have had to come here more than 'a

month or two earlier,' " she told him, "if you wanted to be at Thross when our loch is frozen over. Loch Thross froze over, the last time, just twenty-three winters ago, my uncle says."

Garth looked at the gleaming snow-topped mountains on the horizon, then back at Kathleen to see if she were joking. He saw she was not.

"But," he expostulated, "clear up here in this part of the Highlands, you're almost as far north as Norway, aren't you? And look at the snow on those peaks! I should think every lake would freeze three feet thick in midwinter."

"Some little shallow ponds freeze over, of course," she said, "and sometimes there's several inches of snow on the ground, for days at a time. But I never saw a Scotch loch that was frozen. I don't think any of the bigger lakes freeze solid across, once in twenty years, not even Loch Katrine, down in the Trossachs, where it's ever so cold in winter."

" 'Katrine,' " he repeated, musingly. "What a musical name! You said your own name is 'Kathleen,' didn't you, Miss Macbeath? That's almost as musical. But I could wish they had named you 'Katrine,' instead—not that it is any of my business," he finished, lamely, as she frowned. "I didn't mean to annoy you."

"Why shouldn't it annoy me," she demanded, "to be told you wish they had named me 'Cattle Thief'? That is what 'Katrine' means. It's a corruption of the old Gaelic word, 'Cateran,' that means 'stealer of cattle.' 'Loch Katrine' means 'Cattle Thieves' Lake.' I thought everyone knew that. Thanks, but I prefer 'Kathleen.' That was my mother's name. Her mother was half Irish. That's where she got the name. For that matter, all the Scots were Irish once, you know. They came over from Ireland and drove out the Picts and settled the country."

"They settled a lot of *our* country, too," said Roy. "And I'm sorry I said I wished you had been named for a cattle thief instead of for your mother. We foreigners are apt to blunder when we are in a strange land. I'll try to be careful. Americans aren't any too well loved in Europe, as it is, and I don't want to do my bit to make them worse disliked."

"They're not much disliked in Scotland, I think," argued Kathleen. "Though I'm told they are, for some reason or other, in most countries. Over here, in the Highlands, I think our only feeling against them is the same feeling a hungry child might have for a boy who eats six big meals a day. We are not rich, as a race, we Scots. And as a race you are supposed to be millionaires, aren't you? Perhaps we envy you more than we should. We Scots are joked about as stingy. We aren't stingy. We are poor. Our country is not fertile, in two regions out of three. We haven't many factories, or many great industries, for our size. We have very little money, many of us, so we must learn to make that money go as far as we can and not throw it away. I don't call that stinginess. Do you?"

"No," he said, puzzled at this new slant on traditional

Scot thrift, "I don't. Thank you for explaining it to me. You have the most beautiful scenery on earth, here, too; hundreds of miles of it. There is a charm and a glamour to it all that gets under my skin. It— Speaking of skins, ours are soaking wet, and here we are at the village where our dry clothes are. May I walk as far as the castle gate; or wouldn't your uncle like it?"

"No," she bade him, maternally severe. "You are not going one step beyond the inn; and there you are going to change at once into dry things and then get warm at the kitchen fire and then lie down and get rested. You must be more done in than you realize. . . . It isn't because my uncle wouldn't like you to come as far as the gates or all the way through them. I think I can prove that to you, later today. Good-by. Come on, Stirling!"

She was gone. He stared after her slenderly strong figure as it breasted the steep castle road, until a keen wind off the snowy mountains reminded him of his wet clothes and of the possibility of pneumonia.

"Still," he told himself, as he mounted to his room, "it was worth it."

He tried to convince himself that he meant it was worth such a chance for the sake of promoting his prospects of obtaining a friendly foothold in the castle. But, at the back of his mind was an irritatingly persistent vision of a girl's face close above his own. And the face was not Phyllis Belden's.

With a gnawing feeling of dishonesty, wholly a stranger to him heretofore, he stripped off his dank clothes, and rubbed himself down vigorously with an armful of the inn's handkerchief-sized towels until his healthy flesh glowed and tingled. Then he climbed into a dry suit.

But all the time he was assuring himself sternly that he had done a wholly legitimate thing in forming Kathleen Macbeath's acquaintance as he had. Also that Phyllis was a million times more attractive than she. Somehow his most solemn self-assurances left him with an annoying, if indefinable, lack of conviction.

CHAPTER SIX

———

In MID-AFTERNOON, a gorilla-built man in faded livery and with a face grotesquely well in keeping with his shape appeared in the open doorway of the inn parlor where Garth was sitting and handed Roy a square envelope.

The envelope and the enclosed sheet of paper were crested. The edges were faintly yellow with age. The handwriting was cramped, but letter-press clear. The American read:

Roy Garth, Esquire,
Goat & Compasses Inn,
Thross.

My dear Sir:

My niece tells me of her meeting with you this morning and of the trifling service she was able to render you in fishing you out of our loch. (I performed a like service for an English tourist who fell into the loch at that same spot, some thirty years ago. He offered me a shilling for having saved his life. I handed it back to him, say-

ing I had not elevenpence in change with me. Also I told him who I was. He apologized, saying he had at first mistaken me for a gilly. I told him the error was mutual, as I had at first mistaken him for a gentleman.)

My niece says you are recovering from a nervous attack—although until then I had not believed Yankee nerve was vulnerable to any attack short of a machine gun's—and that the Goat & Compasses is a vile abode for any man, sick or well. In this last statement I concur.

Briefly, she declares our Highland hospitality is shamed by our allowing you to convalesce in such a hole. She has been arguing that point with much earnestness, with me, for some hours. While she has in no way convinced me that I owe hospitality to anyone outside my own clan, yet my sole known weakness is a certain reluctant tenderness for her and an aversion to making her unhappy—a weakness for which I apologize (to myself, not to you).

Also, I am well aware that she is lonely here and that a guest of her own generation may brighten life for her. Perhaps I am influenced even more in your favor by her telling me the astounding fact that my collie, Stirling, proffered friendship to you—a thing he has done hitherto to none save herself and me.

Pardon a prosy old man for the foregoing windy preamble and I will come to the point.

As you wished to see the interior of my home and as my niece thinks we owe something to "the stranger within our gates," I have the honour, my dear sir, to in-

vite you to take up your quarters here at Macbeath Castle during such remaining time as you may decide to sojourn in Thross.

My porter, who bears this invitation, has my command to bring your luggage to the castle. Follow him at your leisure. We dine at eight, but my niece hopes you may arrive in time for tea, at five-fifteen.

I am, my dear sir, yr ob't servant,

CALUM MACBEATH.

Roy read and reread the odd invitation. Half of his brain was madly jubilant at the swift success of his plot. But the other half was still weighted down with that inexplicable sensation of shame.

Angrily, he assured himself that he was doing nothing dishonorable or mean and that he sought only a fair chance to offer the Macbeath a sum for the collie which was far beyond the real cash value of any dog. Surely that was not dishonorable. Moreover, it was the first step toward the fulfilling of his mission to Scotland—the fulfillment which was to bring him home in victory to Phyllis.

But, once more, this once rapturous prospect failed to give him the proper thrill of delight. And again, for no reason at all, he seemed to see two boyishly honest and unafraid brown eyes looking down into his from a flushed little bronzed face.

"Weel," grunted the apelike porter, "d'ye speir to find mair in the bit letter, frae yer second readin'? Wull ye mebbe e'en be giein' yer answer?"

Running up to his room, Garth scribbled a line of thanks and acceptance to the Laird, then handed his note to the porter and began hurriedly to pack his two big suitcases.

At five o'clock he followed his luggage up the steeply winding rock road to Macbeath Castle.

The porter let him in through the clanging old iron gates, whose rusted portcullis spikes and grill yet hung in the vaulted gray archway above. Across a broken flagged courtyard he walked in the porter's wake, toward twin battered carved oak front doors which were opened by a thickset butler in shabby black as the guest drew near.

Garth had a glimpse of a dim-lit stone hall with groined windows and diamonded panes and trophy-hung dark walls and a stone floor. At the hall's far end twinkled a hearth fire in an enormous chimneypiece. Deerskin rugs were strewn over the cold flagging. Ancient and blackened furniture was distributed sparsely about the wide chamber. The place breathed an atmosphere of stately shabbiness and long-vanished magnificence. Its damp chilliness smote Roy like a blow.

From a deep settle alongside a tea table, by the hearth, Kathleen Macbeath sprang up and came forward to greet him, both hands outstretched in friendly welcome.

"You're none the worse for your dip?" she asked.

"Did you catch cold?" he inquired in the very same breath.

Again they broke into that laugh of good-fellowship, at their own simultaneously volleyed questions. And, as before, the laugh seemed to bridge vast chasms of formal acquaintanceship.

"Will you see your room first, or will you wait till you've had tea?" she went on. "The kettle's aboil."

"The room can wait more comfortably than the tea," he replied, lowering himself to the settle across from hers. "What a glorious old hall!" he went on, his eyes roving curiously about the dim spaces and studying as best they could the tattered banners and arms trophies and stag heads on the smoke-darkened walls. "I feel as if I ought to be wearing armor or kilts and shouting, 'Ho, minion!' to some seneschal or justiciar. Not that I know exactly what either a justiciar or a seneschal may happen to be."

"It's a dear old place," said Kathleen. "I love every inch of it. But I was afraid, to a stranger, it might seem perhaps a—well, a bit bleak. Does it?"

He turned his eyes from the grim walls and groined roof and they rested on her eagerly hospitable face and on the firelight that flickered over her.

"No," he made truthful reply, from his very heart. "No, it doesn't. I think you know it doesn't."

Into the room came a maidservant, with a tray whereon were hot scones and thin-sliced bread-and-butter. In through the door the maid had left ajar behind her stepped the red-gold collie, the firelight turning his rich coat to burnished copper. With stately aloofness Stirling followed the servant in, contriving to give the impression that a stray scrap of scone or of buttered bread was the very farthest thing from his thoughts.

At sight of Garth the dog stiffened momentarily, and made as if to withdraw. Then he caught fuller sight and scent of his new-found friend. With plumed tail waving, the collie trotted up to the guest in eager comradeship, pressing against Roy's knee and reveling in the rough rumpling of his head and ears by the guest.

"A cousin of ours," said Kathleen, watching the scene as she paused in her pouring of the tea—"a cousin of ours came here last month, to spend the day. He tried to rumple Stirling's ears like that. Before I could warn him he had a slash that laid his arm open almost from the elbow to the wrist. Yet Stirling loves to have *you* do that to him. Have you a magic with dogs?"

"Not that I know of," laughed Garth, breaking off a corner of buttered scone and tossing it to Stirling. "But I like them a lot and I was brought up with collies. Not with any that were half as magnificent as Stirling, though. I've never seen anything like him. Does your uncle take him to the big dog shows in Scotland or in England?"

"Don't ask uncle that!" she cried, in horror. "He would have an apoplectic stroke. He would no more profane his beloved Stirling by exhibiting him in public than you'd strike a match on the face of the Venus de Milo. No, Stirling is an institution, not a show dog. He's the very last of his wonderful race; the race that began with Harailt, the collie of old King Macbeth's son, Hamish. That's what worries uncle."

"What worries him? I don't—"

"Because there are no Harailt dogs to follow Stirling. The race will die out with him. Uncle is afraid the Luck will die out with him, too. ('The Luck of the Laird,' it's called hereabouts.) Don't laugh, please. Up here we're absurdly superstitious, nearly all of us. There is an old rhymed prophecy about the Harailt dogs. It runs something like this:

" *'MacBheathaig's dog makes safe MacBheathaig's place Till goes from thence the last dog of the race.'*

"Uncle worries over that—not that his own luck is so very good—even while he pretends to laugh at the folly of superstition."

Garth's gaze roamed once more about the shabby old hall whose every scant furnishing cried aloud of dead glories and of present harsh poverty. No, assuredly, "The Luck of the Laird" did not seem to be working at its best, collie or no collie.

Yet, Roy took to heart the girl's speech about Macbeath's fear lest his luck, such as it was, might depart if Stirling should be taken away; and the fear augured little of hope for the success of Garth's efforts to make him sell Stirling.

On his way north, Roy had stopped for an hour to view Stirling Castle, the rock-crowning ancient fortress which so long guarded the Scottish Lowlands against Highland raiders and which was once the key to the whole country. He remembered the proverb, "*Who holds Stirling holds Scotland.*" The phrase took on a curious personal trend to him as he petted the head of the great collie and mused on his own ever-diminishing hopes of buying him.

"I'm wondering if you'd care to stop in at the study and meet my uncle, on the way to your room," suggested Kathleen, as Roy set down his empty teacup. "You must forgive him for not coming down here to meet you. He seldom comes to tea. And this afternoon he has been busy over a pile of mortgages and deeds and the like. He said he would meet you at dinner. But perhaps you wouldn't mind our dropping in on him, as you go upstairs. I'm sure he must have gotten through the worst of his work by now."

She led the way to a narrow passage which ran from the main hall toward a wing of the castle, beneath the turret. Roy followed her, Stirling bringing up the rear. She stopped in front of an iron-studded oaken door of great thickness, and rapped with the carven knocker which hung between its panels.

A scarce-heard command to enter penetrated through the almost soundproof door. Kathleen swung wide the cumbrous portal and they went in.

Roy found himself in a room perhaps a third as spacious as the hall and not dissimilar in look and furnishings. But here there was no vaulted ceiling. Instead, the ceiling was not more than twelve or fourteen feet high; and it was of an unmarred dirty gray. It sagged oddly toward the middle. The windows went up squarely through it, with no embellishment at the top.

In the room's center was a wide Jacobean table, heaped with musty papers. At it, in a gigantic chair, sat the Macbeath, his shoulders hunched over his work. His face wore an egregiously sour aspect. Roy could guess that the strenuous afternoon's toil had dealt with the Laird's mountainous debts and with his futile efforts to stem the demands for payment.

The Macbeath glanced up impatiently. By manifest effort he banished from his ivory-white face the frown caused by the interruption. He got to his feet and came forward with hand outstretched in civil salutation to the guest.

"I make you welcome to Macbeath Castle, Mr. Garth," he said with Old World formality. "My home is yours so long as you may care to honor me and mine by making it so."

The words were as gracious as they were patently insincere. Even while he spoke, the Laird looked furtively toward his swirl of interrupted work on the table.

"It was good of you to let me inflict myself on you, like this, sir," returned Garth. "Thank you for your Christian charity to a very lonely exile, very far from home, Mr.—Lord— Forgive me," he broke off, in boyishly frank perplexity, "but it just occurs to me I haven't the faintest idea whether to call you 'Mister' or 'Sir Calum' or 'Lord Macbeath.' Will you take pity on my American ignorance of titles and tell me?"

"I have no title," replied Macbeath. "So your expansive ignorance need not trip you up, this time. The fifteenth Baron Macbeath—or MacBheathaig—was such a laughably poor gambler as to throw in his fortunes with one Charles Edward Louis Philip Casimir Stuart—Bonnie Prince Charlie, if you care for silly and unmerited nicknames—in the uprising of 1745. He was one of many otherwise sane Scots whose foolish sense of loyalty made him lose more by the Prince's defeat at Culloden than he had had any reason of hoping to gain if the Prince had been victorious. By court influence and by diligent bribery of the right officials, my ancestor was allowed to keep his bare acres and a small part of his remaining fortune—to say nothing of his stupid head—but he was dropped from the British peerage. His descendants have borne no higher title than 'Mister,' except, of course, among their own peasantry, who still insist senselessly on worshiping each successive one of us as the Chief or the Laird."

"Bonnie Prince Charlie!" sighed Kathleen. "I would rather have died in his cause than have won in any other. I can't be sorry that my ancestor staked everything for his sake and lost. I would have done the same thing, I know. He—"

"So I have heard you say before now," grated her uncle, savagely. "And so I've heard many an otherwise normal Hielander say. And it is all poppycock. Your Bonnie Prince Charlie was no man to be worth dying for or risking a clipped penny for. (Few are, for that matter.) He took romantic hold on foolish folk's imaginations, through no merit of his own. Of all the fickle and worthless Stuart line, he was the worst. He was no story-book hero. He was a fat, dissolute, hypocritical coward."

"But," ventured Garth, as Kathleen winced, "wasn't he—?"

"He let his friends impoverish themselves for him, while he stole their decent daughters and spent their hard-won gold pieces," snarled on the Laird. "He ran like a yelping mongrel cur from Culloden field, and he left his loyal dupes to die there for his worthless sake. He would not so much as lead a clan of them into action when he was begged to. He hung back and let them do the fighting for him, and the suffering and the dying. Bonnie Prince Charlie? Losh! The English did well to wipe him and his race off their throne. It is only a few of us maudlin Scots who have made a hero of the fat craven. At that, even if Charles Stuart had been the braw hero the poets claim he was, my ancestor would still have been a fool. Loyalty is the worst failing a human can have. I take shame to him for risking anything for anyone but himself. I could have taught him better. . . . But I'm boring you, Mr. Garth. Also, I'm keeping you from seeing your room—not that that is any cruel deprivation—and you are keeping me from my work, which is as much a deprivation to my creditors as to myself. Shall we say good-by, till dinner?"

He waved his visitors toward the door, then prepared

to reseat himself at the paper-piled table. But his eye was caught by Stirling. The collie had followed Roy into the study and stood now close beside the American, with Garth's hand resting on his head. The Macbeath stared in open surprise. But all he said was:

"The most worshipful devotion I have ever known a dog to lavish on any human was given by a collie down near Pitlochry to a professional sheep-thief who strangled his own father. I'll see you at dinner, Mr. Garth."

As Roy left the study and turned toward the wide stone stairs in the wake of the butler, Kathleen said:

"I hope you will be warm enough, Mr. Garth. I have read that you Americans like to have your rooms as hot as sixty or sixty-five degrees. Of course you can't find that anywhere over here, as you'll know by this time. And I'm afraid you'll find your room chilly, though a peat fire has been burning there ever since we knew you were coming. The only really warm room we have is the study. Uncle hates cold. He spends most of his time in the study, so he found a way of making it warmer. I saw you looking at its ceiling. That isn't a ceiling at all. It is canvas that Uncle had stretched across, when he was a young man. The real ceiling is fifteen feet higher. But he keeps the heat from rising by that lower ceiling of canvas."

Roy paid no special heed to the words, at the time, except that they explained to him why the supposed stone ceiling sagged so in the middle. He was to have much reason to recall the trivial fact.

Left alone in the study, Macbeath went back to his paper-littered table. He shoved aside a clutter of faded and yellow deeds and mortgages and similar documents of varying ages, as well as a sheet crossed and crisscrossed with penciled figures.

Thence he exhumed a page of crested writing paper on which he had been scribbling when Garth and Kathleen came in. Now, dipping his rusty pen afresh in the inkhorn, the Laird resumed his writing. The letter was addressed to his solicitor at Perth. Macbeath took up the labor of continuing it, in mid-sentence.

—upshot of it all is, my dear Hughie, that on the twelfth inspection of my affairs they are as badly muddled as on the first. "Muddled" is perhaps a misnomer. For they are crystal-clear. They may be summed up, thus: I owe everything and I own nothing. I am at the tail end of every resource. I have drained every possible cash channel. Indeed, I have drained everything save my creditors' capacity. I can hold them off no longer.

Yet it is a case of "going down in sight of port." For if only I could lay my hands on some fourteen or fifteen hundred pounds, to stave off the next quarter's payments and to toss a few guineas, on account, into the gaping mouths of one or two of the more threatening of the creditor pack—if only I had in hand some fifteen hundred guineas, at very most—the day would be saved.

For you say your colleague's American syndicate will have its experts here by July, to look into the coal pros-

*pects at Wat's Ness. Hughie, I shall see to it that they
find coal in strong enough traces to make them advise
buying. And for all I know there may actually be coal
down there. If it is there or not, now, it will be there by
July. Once let them find the right signs of it, and the
syndicate will buy.*

*That will mean snug comfort, and cessation from eter-
nal money-worry. At least, it would if July were tomorrow and not four leaden-legged months off. Before July,
it will be too late. As you hint so diplomatically in your
honoured favor of last Tuesday, there's not another
clipped penny to be begged or borrowed or commandeered, by me, anywhere. I shall be cleaned out, sold
out, driven out, long before July. Oh, for the sweet old
days when a Hieland gentleman might lead a band of
his loyal clansfolk to the slaughter of his creditors!*

*There is a thick-brained young Yankee visiting us. I
understand he is as rich in dollars as he is poor in mental-
ity. I shall sound him, as I find chance, on Scottish investments. Those men with money and no brains are sent
on earth for the salvation of those with brains and no
money. At least, it can do no harm for me to try to interest him in leaving some of his burden of wealth here with
me. It is not as if he were a fellow-Scot or even an Eng-
lishman. The laws of hospitality—so far as they concern
myself—stop dead short on the eastern verge of the Atlantic. The law is off on Crœsuses from the States. So I
shall try.*

By the bye, kindly incorporate the following items in

a codicil to my will, and draw it up and send it to me to sign. The less cash I have, the more I want to bequeath other treasures to my legatees. Here are the notes I have jotted:

To my nephew, Gordon Macbeath, I give and bequeath the rare privilege of earning his own living. He has been going on the theory, since his father's death, that this is a pleasure reserved for me alone. I beg to call his attention to the fact that he is mistaken in his simple faith.

To my valet, Comas McCuen, I bequeath the remnant of my wardrobe which he has been working so industriously to demolish for the past eight years. This includes my best silk hat—the one he always wears to church when I am from home.

To my bailiff, Peter Ochilvie, I bequeath the farm machinery which he has almost ruined through his awkward ignorance and his neglect. I leave to him the pleasing task of completing what he has so finely begun.

To my solicitor, Hugh McBain Douglas, I bequeath the advice to get as quickly as possible another client whom he can bleed as profitably as always he has bled me.

"To my—"

Kathleen rapped at the heavy door. Macbeath slipped the letter beneath the other papers and bade her enter.

"There is only one bottle of the 1867 port left," reported the girl. "Will that be enough, do you think, at dinner?"

"It will be just one bottle more than enough," decreed Macbeath. "No, on second thought, serve the port, and have brandy served in here with the coffee. I shall want to soften his heart and then talk of business to him. Now run along. I am busy. Or perhaps I am only fidgety. It is often the same thing."

When, at eight, Garth descended the big stairway, clad for dinner, he found the hall softly lighted by some fifty wax candles of differing lengths, in sconces along the wall. Their mellow radiance flooded the aged room and brought into warm relief the glint of sword or spear or battle-ax on the walls and the sheen of ancient silver on the black refectory table in front of the hearth.

Kathleen looked up from her task of arranging early primroses and violets in a copper dish in mid-table as Roy came in.

"The village people seem bent on regarding your visit to the castle as something of an Event with a capital E," she hailed him, gaily. "For two hours they have been bringing flowers and food and all manner of things to the postern. Two of them brought a fawn, all dressed and ready to roast. Another brought two brace of pheasant and a hare and a brace of grouse—though everyone knows it is a jail offense to kill deer or any form of game in March. And Dugal—he's the hereditary clan piper—insists on donning kilts and playing for us, this evening. He says he has composed 'a graund chune' in honor of our foreign guest. He—"

"I'm rather overwhelmed," answered Roy, noting the tender flickering of the candle flames on her bright hair and white muslin evening dress. "Besides, I don't understand. During the day or two I spent at the inn, nobody—"

"Oh," she explained, "down there, you were only a tourist—a 'tripper,' as they're called. Something to be tolerated for the money you brought into the village. Here, you're the Laird's honored guest. That means the clan must do you honor, too, as long as you stay here. It's immemorial custom. Family pride, I suppose. According to tradition, the chief is always 'cousin' to every member of his clan. And gifts must be brought to his guest."

She did not add that these gifts—such of them as were edible—had been mightily welcome in re-enforcing an over-lean larder. The venison and pheasants and hare and grouse, as well as offerings of eggs and cream and vegetables and flitches of bacon, had helped to solve a grave problem of feeding a guest who could not reasonably be asked to share the household's ordinary Spartan fare.

Before she could say more the Macbeath came down from his dressing room. Roy Garth stared unashamedly at his host. His own well-cut dinner clothes seemed all at once ugly and insignificant compared to the Laird's sartorial splendor.

The Macbeath was in Highland full dress, of a half-century agone and of a style in vogue five hundred years back. In full plaid and kilts, bare of knee and with his clan's dress tartan caught at the shoulder by a massy silver-and-cairngorm brooch, he might well have stepped straight out of one of Scott's novels. From his baldric swung a furred sporran and from his hip hung a long black-and-silver-scabbarded dress-dirk. From the top of one of his brown plaided socks, below the bare and wizened knee, peeped the cairngormed hilt of the regulation *sgian dhu* (black dagger). In every detail he was a Highland thane of Macbeth's own time.

Oddly enough, there was nothing grotesque, nothing ludicrous, in his appearance. The ancestral garb was strangely becoming to him, setting off his gaunt figure and fierce white face. It was Garth who appeared ill-dressed and out of place there, in the grim candle-lit stone hall; not the hall's hereditary owner.

"I always choose to dress for dinner after the fashion of a Hieland gentleman," said Macbeath, stiffly, noting Garth's instantly averted stare of amazement. "I trust it may help your search of local color."

"It's—stunning!" cried Garth, in sudden impulse of admiration.

"It's customary," gravely corrected his host.

He crossed to the head of the board, though the meal had not been announced, and seated himself without waiting for his niece or his guest to be seated. He did it with no show of rudeness, but calmly, as if by right.

There was a certain majesty in the action. To Garth's mental vision it evoked a picture of a hundred retainers and lesser chieftains and women of the household, standing respectfully about a long board in this same hall, waiting until the chief should seat himself at the table's head. To his memory came the historic boast of Rob Roy MacGregor:

"Wherever MacGregor sits is the head of the table!"

No longer did the brag seem pompous or ridiculous.

CHAPTER SEVEN

———

THE butler drew back Kathleen's chair, opposite her uncle's. A second man in painfully ill-fitting and unaccustomed shabby livery drew back Roy's. Apparently he had been drafted from the village or from some clan farm, for this novel service.

The dinner began. Kathleen talked pleasantly with Roy on various indifferent topics, Macbeath throwing in a carelessly sardonic word here and there. A handful of spring blooms slipped from place, in a massive silver loving cup, near the center of the table. Kathleen bent forward to readjust them.

"That cup," volunteered Macbeath, as Garth looked interestedly at the vessel's antique carving—"that cup belonged to the Baron Macbeath I told you of—he who fought for the so-called Bonnie Prince Charlie. It was one of the few pieces of his heavier family plate that he did not melt down to get funds for the Pretender's half-starved army. You know the origin of the loving cup, do you not, with its three handles? It was devised here in Scotland. The Hieland host was supposed to hold two of the three handles while he offered it to his guest to drink from. This, so that the guest might be comfortably sure his host would not stab him while he was drinking. A very necessary precaution in the bad good old days."

"Not really?"

"Why, my own sweet ancestor, Macbeth, is even credited with killing his guest and sovereign, King Duncan, in the castle on whose site this castle of mine stands! You've seen it in the playhouses, perhaps? But I think that was one of Shakespeare's lies. You see, King James I of England—the first English Stuart—was Shakespeare's patron, and James was descended from Duncan. So, to curry favor with his fat-headed royal patron, Shakespeare made Macbeth a villain, and made Duncan and his son Malcolm holy heroes. And thus it will cling in the public mind forever, even though history says Macbeth was something of a good and wise king—for his day. One interesting lie can always kill a hundred truths. And, speaking of liars: At Inverness one black-fog night I collided with a man in the street. (It was so foggy I couldn't tell if he was a short man with whiskers or a tall man with a sporran.) And the first word he spoke to me—"

The chief was interrupted by a most ungodly sound. Down the candle-lit hall strutted a truly impressive figure, moving rhythmically toward the table. As he came within the radius of candle-glow, he resolved himself into an aged and red-faced man, bearded and bald, swathed in a flaming faded tartan. His cheeks were swelled out, as though with mumps, from his heroic efforts at blowing into a dropsical pair of immense bag-pipes.

This evidently was Dugal, the clan piper of whose advent Kathleen had warned Garth. Up to the table he marched, then made a half turn and proceeded to strut back and forth in the open space between board and hearth, puffing lustily at his pipes.

To Garth's unaccustomed senses, the ensuing sound was earsplittingly hideous. But Macbeath listened to the tuneless cacophony with a manifestly approving delight, while Kathleen seemed to enjoy it fully as well. Therefore Roy steeled his face to expressionlessness, and strove to remain tranquil as the piper belched forth his volume of droning and squeaking and skirling discord.

"I think I know, now," mused Garth, as the playing and the strutting continued—"I think I know now why a bagpiper always keeps moving while he pipes. It's to disturb the aim of anyone who may try to shoot him."

Stirling, lying at the hearthside, did not share his master's enjoyment of the shrieking din. For, after fidgeting and growling softly for a minute or two, he lifted his chiseled head and turned the bagpipe solo into a deafening duet by giving vent to a dolorously long-drawn howl of protest.

"Quiet, Stirling!" rasped the Laird, annoyed by the sacrilegious interruption to his loved music.

Stirling obeyed. But with much dignity he got up from the hearth and came aggrievedly over to Roy Garth; standing beside the American, his head in the latter's lap, during the rest of the performance. He seemed to sense a fellow-sufferer, in this foreign guest; and chose to come close to him, that they might endure their enforced aural martyrdom together.

At last the awful solo was ended, dying down in a droning diminuendo such as might issue from the throat of an expiring cow.

Remembering that Kathleen said the piper had composed this "graund chune" in the stranger's honor, Garth mumbled his thanks and wondered whether or not it would be all right for him to tip the fellow.

But the Macbeath was loud and eager in his praise. The dour old Laird had actually been galvanized into a flash of human enthusiasm.

"Hech, Dugal!" he cried, his thin voice as high and shrill as the pipes themselves. "*Slainté!*" He filled a goblet with raw whiskey and shoved it toward the red and perspiring piper, then filled another for himself.

"*Slainté agadsa!*" he shrilled. "*Air do slainté! Uisge beatha?*" ("Thanks! A health to you! Some whiskey?")

Gravely Dugal accepted the brimming goblet of raw spirit from his chief. Gravely he lifted it on high. Then, intoning: "*Slainté na Righ! Slainté na duin uasal!*" ("Health to the king and health to this gentleman!") he swigged the fire-potent half pint of whiskey at a single appreciative gulp. Then he dashed the glass down upon the hearthstone, saluted, and swaggered consequentially from the hall.

To hear a band of regimental pipers as they march down from the Castle Rock at Edinburgh—to listen to the skirl of fifty pipes as they measure the tread of armed men through wynd and highway—these are experiences which thrill the veriest outlander with a strange ecstasy. But to listen to an improvised lilt or coronach, played by a solitary brass-lunged piper beneath an echoing vaulted roof—one must be a born and ancestored Scot to endure it without dismay.

Garth understood now the depths of significance in the Gilbertian appeal to McCann, the piper; and under his breath he misquoted savagely:

> "*Or if you* MUST *play on the cursed affair,*
> *At least grind out something resembling an air!*"

With difficulty he pulled himself together.

"That's something I shan't forget," he made shift to say. "It is the first and only time a tune has been composed and played in my honor. I appreciate it more than I can say. I wish I could have thanked him more adequately."

Macbeath's smoldering black eyes were looking him through and through.

"Which is a polite way," the Laird commented, dryly, "of saying it is the most excruciating agony your ears ever underwent. Bagpipe music like that is the grandest melody on earth. But one must be a Hielander for at least ten generations back to appreciate it and love it. I commend your courtesy, young sir, more than I can commend your veracity. Still, it—"

Through the open window, from the courtyard below, issued a sudden yowling, varied with spittings and growls.

"Dugal is serenading us from outside?" politely queried Garth as Stirling ran barking toward the casement.

"No," replied Kathleen, purple with repressed mirth and not daring to glance at her uncle. "No, those are cats fighting. The sound is just a very little like Dugal's pipes. But it's only cats."

" 'Cats wha hae?' " suggested Roy, by way of shifting the unfortunate subject.

His frightful pun's only result was a murmured snarl from the Laird:

"Men have been shot for less!"

The dinner ended as constrainedly as it had begun merrily. The men went into the study for their coffee, Stirling following them, while Kathleen wandered into a tiny room across the passage, and sat down at an ancient square piano whose worn-out notes were mere melodious whispers.

Much Garth wished he might have gone thither with her; but he knew he must needs follow his host. In the study, Macbeath by palpable effort talked entertainingly, if without any pretence of interest in what he was saying.

Roy chanced to notice a pair of rusted swords with long straight blades and basket hilts, crossed on the wall, at the room's far end. Macbeath lifted the desk lamp and thus brought the weapons into clearer view.

"Those were the two claymores my ancestor used during the Prince Charlie campaign of 1745," said he. "That one to the left he fought with at Preston Pans, and he split the skull of a dismounted English dragoon captain with it. The second one he wielded at Culloden. He used to claim that he ran two Lowlanders through with it, and sliced the face of a third, in that sorry fight. Probably he lied. It was a habit of his."

He set down the lamp. The scabbard of his dress dirk caught against his chair arm as he sat down. The dirk and the scabbard fell loose to the floor.

"This belonged to him, also," he went on. "Though I keep it cleaner than the claymores, as it is a part of my evening dress. The Hielanders went into battle with the targe, or shield, on the left arm and with the long dirk in the left hand. They wielded the claymore in the right hand. In the sock or the boot was stuck this short *sgian dhu*. This was only for use when a man was beaten to his knees or when he was forced to kneel for mercy to a stronger foe. Then he would drop to his knee, and at the same time he would whip out his *sgian dhu* and drive it into the enemy's abdomen. Almost as sportsmanly an act as stabbing the guest as he drank, was it not?"

"You're joking, of course!" laughed Garth.

"That is a luxury I do not permit myself," denied the Laird. "Moreover, so foreigners say, joking is not a Scottish vice. I was speaking of the olden days as they *were*; not as you moderns see them through a rose-mist of Sir Walter's poetry and Bruns's songs. Not that there was not glamour, too, I suppose. All the Hielands are heavy-hung with glamour and with romance of a sort. Our very lochs are liquid history. You can testify to the liquid quality of at least one of them."

"I can, indeed," assented Roy, again vexed at the pang of shame that pricked him as he recalled the ruse whereby he had won Kathleen's acquaintance. "But when you speak of men who knelt to a winning enemy in order to stab him and of hosts who stabbed their guests when they were drinking—"

"The life of any mountaineer is stern and rough," expounded the Laird, "even as the religion of a mountaineer people is stern and compelling. That has ever been so. The Hielanders, of old, as ever since, lived in a lean country. Thus their souls could not put on flesh. They were at grips with realities. Love was love. Hate was hate. Need was dire need. Strong men took what they would. Weak men kept what they could. This is true Nature, is it not?"

"I suppose so," agreed Garth, reluctantly, "yet there is such a thing as civilization and as humanity and—"

"When life is soft enough to permit of them, yes. But when a Hieland chief was bone-poor and when he saw his 'cousins'—his clansfolk—going hungry, and when he knew a fat lowland lord had fat cattle and fat storehouses of grain, can you sneer at him for leading his hungry clan on a foray into that fat man's fat country? Or, when there seemed fair chance of success in raiding some Hieland enemy's pastures, was it not nature for him to do it, and then for the enemy to retaliate, and for a very pretty mountaineer internecine war to follow? You call it Theft. They called it Custom. And, after all, was it so much more confiscatory than your own income tax or Great Britain's? Then, as now, the strong ate the weak. You must pay your heavy income tax, because the government is stronger than you are. The weak farmer, in a weak clan, must pay out his steers because the raider was stronger than he."

"But surely the chief—"

"The chief was chief only because he could look after the welfare of his clan. His men saw to it that his life was not too much easier than theirs. My own great-great-grandfather was encamped with his followers on the crest of Ben Thross, in a campaign. It was bitter midwinter weather. He rolled a lump of snow for a pillow, as he and his men laid them down to sleep on the frozen ground. His body servant kicked away the snow pillow and yelled to him:

" 'D'ye speir to lie saft, we' a fine cushion for yer heid, the while yer cousins maun lay their ain heids on stanes?'

"Yes, they were hard folk, those old Hieland men— hard and practical. They had to get the fullest value out of each penny and out of every other possession, if they did not wish to starve. Here is an instance:"

The Laird drew from his belt the long, black-scabbarded dirk that was an integral part of his evening garb. Two small handles protruded along its sheath. One after another Macbeath pulled at these handles, displaying to Roy's amused gaze a tiny meat knife and a two-tined fork.

"They are part of every true Hieland dirk," said Macbeath as he shoved them back into their sockets in the sheath. "And many a laugh have they caused from foreigners. But they served hungry soldiers as knife and fork, on campaign meals; and they saved those same idealistic soldiers from the ignominy of profaning an honorable war dirk by the sordid cutting up of food. There you see the mingled practicality and idealism of my people."

Macbeath checked himself, as if fearing his guest might be bored by the long disquisition. With abrupt shift of theme, he said:

"By the way, you came to Scotland to rest, I understand. You did not come on business?"

Though the question was carelessly asked, yet no longer was there a dearth of interest in the dry old voice. The black eyes under the penthouse of black brows were fixed keenly on the guest's face.

Roy suppressed a start at the illogical fear lest Macbeath's uncanny old brain might have guessed the real object of his visit. Steadying his voice, he answered in a tone as elaborately careless as his host's:

"Most men are glad of a chance to do any sort of advantageous business, aren't they, whether they are on vacation or not? At least it is so in America."

"I asked," resumed Macbeath, guardedly, "because American capital could do so much to develop this rich region of ours. For example, I have acres and miles of land that would respond richly to money and wise care. Water power—mines in my hills—moors to let for the shooting—"

His old voice died away and a faint red smeared the ivory white of his parchment-like skin. Roy understood. He knew this ancient Scot had only saturnine contempt for him and for the outside world at large. He knew that Macbeath's civility toward him was assumed with painful difficulty. And now he knew one reason why he had been asked to the castle.

The Laird's debts and duns must have become unbearably pressing before the crabbed aristocrat could set himself to the task of angling shamelessly for American money, and could smirch his own hospitality for the hope of gain. Roy recalled what Kathleen had said about all Americans being fabulously rich. Probably he himself was supposed to be a plutocrat, from the fact that he had traveled so far on what appeared to be a mere health tour.

If Macbeath were so terribly in need of money, perhaps it was not impossible, after all, that the Laird might listen to a gilt-edged offer for his peerless collie.

Even a very few thousand dollars might be a godsend to him; as his debts and his needs ringed him in closer and closer.

Yawning politely behind his hand, Garth waited for the chief's next move. His other hand, as if by idle chance, dropped to the head of the collie that lay beside his chair.

"I asked," continued Macbeath, "because every good patriot is interested in attracting to his homeland the prosperity and trade and industries of other and richer countries. If I can be of use in the investing of any capital you may feel like staking here, in the very certain hope of large returns—"

Again the old voice trailed away into silence. The man was in evident mental agony, in his hated and ill-fitting role of promoter. Roy judged the psychic moment had come.

"I am afraid," he said, in courteous but firm regret— "I am afraid I would not be interested in any investments outside of the United States. I am somewhat hidebound in that way. At least," he went on, whimsically, as he bent down again to pat Shirling's upraised head—"at least, there is only one thing I have seen up here that tempts me, as an investor."

"Yes?" eagerly croaked the Macbeath, leaning forward. "Yes?"

"Just a whim of mine, of course," laughed Garth, with a self-tolerant air, "but I am glad to pay well for my whims. And I would pay—well, I would gladly pay ten thousand dollars, in ready cash, for the sake of gratifying that one petty whim. Ten thousand dollars may not seem a large sum to you, sir," he said, deprecatorily, "but it is no more and no less than I am willing to pay. Spot cash, at that. No note and no installments."

He relighted his cigar, affecting not to see the glow of craving that was hidden so quickly behind the bushy Mephistophelean brows at mention of the huge sum.

"And," queried Macbeath, trying with pitiful ill-success to mask his eagerness in flippancy, "and what may be the precious object that has wakened this 'whim' of yours? Ten thousand dollars seems a fair-sized sum to pay for the gratifying of whims. But perhaps you are a man of iron whims. That is your affair, not mine. What might it be—if the question is not impertinent from an old man to a young? A lease on one of my shooting moors? Or—"

"I would gladly pay ten thousand dollars—spot cash —ten thousand dollars, *down*, no more, no less," answered Roy, "for this collie of yours. Will you sell him to me for that?"

It was out! It was said! Garth's heart stood still. He tried not to pant. The die was cast.

He glanced across questioningly at his host.

Macbeath's harsh-lined face went almost inanely blank. Then of a sudden a startling change rushed over it.

If possible it went more corpse-white than before; the slanting black brows standing out like accent-shaped ink strokes. The black eyes ceased to smolder, and blazed into an all but maniacal fire.

Twice the Laird essayed to speak, as he leaped trembling to his feet and stood towering above his guest. But the words gushed forth inaudible and like the snarl of a rabid beast.

His fist tightened convulsively about the silver-and-black-banded hilt of the murderous long dirk he wore; the grim dirk with the immemorially grotesque tiny knife and fork stuck into the side of its scabbard.

The withering glare of the flaming old eyes cut into

the very soul of the man who sat trying to look serenely up at the transfigured Highlander. Thus, thought Roy, might the original Macbeth have glared down at King Duncan ere he slew his royal guest.

In a none-too-successful effort at indifference Garth glanced away from the enraged chief. His eyes chanced to rest on a shield-shaped mirror that hung behind the writing table. Its glass reflected himself there, and a small space directly behind him.

Garth's first idle gaze at this narrowed space focused suddenly into horror. Forgotten was the raging Macbeath and everything else; as Roy stared breathless into the telltale glass.

A numbing chill assailed him. For the moment he was helpless to move or even to cry out.

CHAPTER EIGHT

GARTH was sitting with his back to the dark-paneled wall and with perhaps a yard of space between him and it. Macbeath, towering lean and homicidal above him, was facing the same bit of panel.

As Roy's glance happened to fall on his own reflection in the shield looking-glass over the table, he had a clear view of the paneling. His eye had been caught by a stealthy motion.

As he gazed he saw the nearest panel begin to slide stealthily open. In the dim space behind it was mirrored a black-clad human arm whose gnarled hand gripped something curved and metallic that flashed back the reading-lamp's rays.

So silent, so unforeseen was the apparition that Garth sat stupefied, paralyzed by a weird sense of horror. He struggled to move, to spring far away from the stealthy menace behind him. But for an instant he could not.

Then, as the panel slid wider, the American shook off his startled numbness. Up he leaped, whirling about, tense, alert, ready to grapple with the mysterious intruder who had come upon him from behind in such ghostly fashion.

A single incredulous glimpse and Roy sank back in his chair, choking with the laughter of sheer reaction, dizzy with relief, ashamed at his own unprecedented fear.

The panel now stood almost wide open, revealing a candle-lit passage to the kitchen wing of the castle. In the opening stood the thickset butler.

In one hand he bore a silver-covered bottle whose sheen caught the lamp's rays. In his other he was balancing two liqueur glasses on a small tray. His foot was still busy pushing wider the panel.

The Macbeath snorted with anger at the retainer's interruption of his blind-fury fit. He favored the luckless and clumsy butler with a murderous glower.

The butler quailed under the glare of his overlord and stammered, apologetically:

"Your lordship—your lordship told me to—to bring the Napoleon brandy into the study here, after the coffee. I— I—"

"Quite," assented Macbeath, with muffled steadiness of tone as he turned away and walked to the farthest end of the room. "Set it down on the table. You may take the coffee things—unless Mr. Garth will have another cup."

"No, thank you," said Garth, swallowing his laughter of reaction. "And I don't think I care for a liqueur."

The butler set down the bottle and the tray, and backed out through the opening, closing the panel behind him as he went. Apparently, at least one of the ancient castle's former secret passageways was utilized in these prosaic modern times as a short cut from pantry to study.

The Laird had begun to pace rapidly up and down the far end of the room, his hands behind him, his head bent. The flame of insensate rage had spent itself. He was sane again—sane and in apparent deep self-communion.

Garth let him pace thus, uninterrupted, for several minutes. Then, feeling the situation was becoming ridiculous, he ventured to say:

"I seem to have annoyed you by offering you ten thousand dollars for this splendid collie of yours. If I have transgressed any local custom by making the offer, I am sorry; and I can only say it was you who started me on it by suggesting that I invest some of my money here. I told you there was only one investment I cared about making in Scotland, and you seemed eager to know what it was. If my answer made you angry, it was my bad luck rather than my fault. I'm densely ignorant of Highland etiquette."

Twice again the Laird strode back and forth without replying. Then he faced his guest once more, coming into the radius of lamplight from the dimness of the far side of the study.

His face had regained its accustomed sardonic composure. His voice was dry and rasping, as ever, and was void of any emotion except polite boredom. Garth gave mute credit to the man's fine power of regaining shattered self-control.

"It is I who should apologize," said Macbeath. "Not you. Up here in the Hielands we outworn relics of another century live too much in the past—in the past that was full of idle superstitions, like wraiths floating hazily in the murk. We do not realize we are in the twentieth century, the age of wireless and airship and radio—and Yankees. We forget the Mid-Victorian Era has given place to the Mid-Vulgarian Age. I shan't forget again."

"But—" began Garth.

The Laird rambled on:

"We forget that of all the myriad uselessly dear things Electricity has slain, its earliest and most complete murder was that of the Past. The Past and Electricity cannot live in the same world. In the Past there was an absurd legend that when the last dog of Stirling's race—the old Harailt line—shall be gone from Macbeath Castle, the Luck of the Laird also will go.

"It was an unbidden memory of our legend which made me behave like an undisciplined schoolboy, just now. I have the intelligence to see that while such legends are trash in this electrical age of yours, ten thousand dollars is a miracle from heaven in all ages and climes. It is a preposterous price to pay for a mere dog. It is even farther beyond the value of the average human. You are quite in earnest in making the offer, Mr. Garth?"

"I am," assented Garth, marveling vastly at the change in his host's manner and outlook. "To prove it, I am ready to hand over to you, at any time you say, ten certified checks on the Bank of England for two hundred pounds sterling each, in return for a bill of sale for your collie. Is that satisfactory? Does it convince you I am in earnest? If not, I am ready to deposit the sum in your nearest bank, to be held in escrow until the deal is closed.

How about it? By the way, to avoid haggling, I repeat that this is my final offer."

Once more the chief did not answer at once; but stood, with eyes all but shut and with lips moving silently as in rapt cogitation. Then he looked at Garth again and said:

"You must give me a few hours to think it over. I can tell you now that I am almost inclined to close with your offer. Inside of twenty-four hours at most I will give you your answer definitely. In return I ask your pledge to say nothing of this to my niece or to anyone. Is it a bargain?"

"Yes," declared Garth, incredulous at his own good luck and at the utter ease wherewith his supposedly ticklish mission promised to be achieved. "Yes. And you'll let me know, definitely, by tomorrow night?"

"By tomorrow night, at latest," agreed Macbeath, adding, courteously: "And now I have kept you for an unconscionable time talking with an uninteresting old man. I forget always that Youth can be entertained only by Youth. Age is selfish. Selfishness, and a wondrous aptitude for inconveniencing everybody younger, are its only remaining joys. Run and talk to my niece, if you like. I have work to finish."

Garth wasted no time in availing himself of the leave to depart. From Belden, long ago, he had learned that a vital rule of salesmanship or of any form of business deal is to know when to end an interview. Thus, he was eager to be gone, lest the Laird change his mind and recant his astoundingly favorable attitude toward the selling of Stirling.

Moreover, before the closing of the heavy study door had shut off all outer sounds, Roy had heard the whisperingly tuneful old square piano tinkle forth the first notes of a familiar Highland air. The player's touch, no less than the piano itself, was in vast and soothing contrast to be vigorously jazzsome racket which used to lure him to Phyllis Belden's music room. He yearned to hear more.

Courteously the Macbeath accompanied his guest to the study threshold, closing the door behind him as Roy went out. Then meditatively the chief went back to his table. In his cryptic black eyes was a twinkle of almost goblin amusement.

But Roy was strolling through a fool's paradise just then. His mind was immeasurably relieved at his new prospects of success. His work was done until Macbeath should give definite acceptance of the offer. He had scope to enjoy to the full his evening with Kathleen.

The girl did not look around as Garth came into the little alcove room where she was playing. Very sweet and very Old World, she looked, just then, in the faint candlelight; her soft white dress bright against the dark background of wall and floor. Her brown eyes were half shut. Her strong young fingers were straying idly over the time-yellowed keys.

Whether she was improvising or whether she was playing from memory some hauntingly sweet old fragment of melody, Roy did not know. But he knew the soft music sank far deeper into his heart than ever had Phyllis's pyrotechnic lambasting of the keys. And again he was aware of an uneasy sense of disloyalty to the girl who was waiting for him in Midwestburg.

To his memory returned a carelessly flippant something Phyllis had said to him during that last unbearably long evening of theirs at Beldencroft.

"I think," she had told him—"I think I'll have to compose a Gaelic march, while you're gone, to greet you with when you come home in triumph with the incomparable Highland dog and all his host of incomparable Highland fleas. It ought to be easy. I read somewhere that all one has to do is to use only the black keys of the piano and to stick to some rudimentary sort of rhythm— and the result is bound to be a Scotch air."

Yet Kathleen's flowingly graceful fingers did not "use only the black keys," nor was she following any rhythm more binding than is that of a catbird's unrehearsed song. The tiny notes whispered and chimed and blended through the dim room. Their spell began to do queerly unaccountable things to the listener's heart-nerves.

The supple fingers ceased to move gently across the keys. Kathleen smiled up at him as he leaned mute and tense over the piano. There was wistful plea for his approval in her lovely level glance.

"What were you playing?" he asked, huskily.

"I don't know," she answered, hesitating as in embarrassment. "It just came to me as I went along. Sometimes it does. I think it was about the moors with the March breeze crooning across them and the primroses coming to life in the lee of the braes. But partly it was about

the tens of thousands of gallant laddies who used to live
on these Hieland moors and who left them desolate."

"Left them? I don't understand."

"In the old days, you know, there were five folk hereabout where there's barely one now. The revolt of 1745
and the punishing, and then the 'hard years' and the call
of America and the scarce food—all those things turned
miles and miles of our sweet Hielands into empty wastes.
It is not a happy thing for any Scot to remember. In your
own country, you live all in the present and in the future.
You don't have to live in the past and to feel so sad over
it sometimes that you find your fingers weaving cor-
onachs about it. Your America is very terribly modern,
isn't it?"

"Perhaps that is why the murk and magic and beauty
of these moors have taken such hold on me," said Roy,
still bending above her, over the piano edge. "They're
bewitching me, I think. We have nothing like them at
home. Perhaps over there we are too up-to-date; though
it never occurred to me that we could be, till I came
here."

"The Hielands are getting more and more up-to-date,
too," she defended her homeland from the imagined
slur. "Even here in Thross, far off the tourist track. For
instance, family after family is stopping the use of tallow
candles for lighting their houses. Dozens have begun using these new-fangled kerosene lamps. And at Ferrol
there is gas at the inn and at the railroad station. Honestly
there is, Mr. Garth. And street lamps at every quarter

mile. And there's running water, in the station hotel. We Hielanders are not so far behind the times, you see. And at Inverness several of the biggest streets are lighted nearly all night."

He did not answer. He did not hear. His mind was on the honest brown eyes upraised to his; and on the strong slender hands whose fingers once more were straying listlessly over the old keys; and on the cadences of her soft Scottish voice.

Roy's conscience upbraided him in hot if belated rebuke, at the all-encompassing interest he was beginning to take in this girl whom he scarcely knew. Yet, for once, he shut his mental ears to the warning. This evening, at least, was his own. He had earned it, and he vowed he would enjoy its strange charm to the full.

"And," continued the girl, suddenly, as she ceased to caress the piano keys and looked up at him in almost childish excitement, "next week, you're going to see another proof that we are up-to-date. At the Spring Holiday Fair. There's going to be a balloon ascent this year. Did you ever see a balloon ascent? They're the very newest thing in fair amusement, Dugal says."

"I— I seem to have heard of them," said Garth, adding: "Only very lately, though. I never went up in a balloon, of course; but I'll be glad to, if you like. It would be a novelty and I could boast about it to my friends who never even heard of such a thing."

"Oh, but people don't go up in it, Dugal says. Not the spectators. It isn't like a six-penny donkey ride. He says the balloon is filled with gas made out of steel filings and vitriol, and then the aeronaut gets aboard and the men let go of the ropes and the balloon goes flying up, clear out of sight. Dugal saw one, at Pitlochry, last spring. He says the balloon is bigger than the turret here; and that it goes up so far that it's only a speck, and then it's nothing at all. The aëronaut must be a brave man."

"Braver than I am, anyhow," confessed Garth. "I always get dizzy and sick at any great height. I envy people who don't. Yes, it must be a wonderful spectacle."

He thrust from his mind the gray memory of infinite boredom which had been his, again and again, as a boy, in watching the tedious balloon ascensions at county fairs at home; in the days before such dull performances lost their last shred of public favor. He would as soon have broken a sick child's one loved toy as to cast a damper on this wide-eyed girl's delight in the prospect of showing him the promised marvel.

"You say it's to be at a fair?" he went on. "Isn't it rather early for outdoor fairs? In America we have them somewhere around September, when the crops are all in and when the farmers have time and spending money to waste. Is——?"

"This is the Spring Holiday Fair," she explained. "It dates back ever so many centuries. Uncle says it's a survival of the old pagan Spring Festival. Anyhow, it is a sacred feature of Hieland life. It is the jolliest thing that happens all year. They have it in a dozen different places, all over. The one we're going to is only a mile or two from here, on the way to Ferrol. Oh dear!" she broke off, in belated recollection. "I was going to keep it a secret and surprise you with it that morning! I wanted to see your face when you came in sight of the balloon. And now I've spoiled it all. I'm—"

"You haven't spoiled it, an atom!" he declared. "You've given me something to look forward to. Besides, I hate surprises. Sometimes it's hard to tell them apart from shocks. And it'll be gorgeous to go to a Highland Fair—with you. Thanks, ever and ever so much. It was *very sweet* of you to think of it for me."

"I'm so glad!" she sighed, happily. "I was afraid it might bore you, after the rush of amusements and excitements all you Americans seem to have at home. Concerts and lectures every week or so, I suppose; and stereopticon views and all that. Of course, I knew the balloon would be thrilling. But I was afraid the rest of it—"

"Every minute of it will be gorgeous fun," he insisted. "That's a prophecy. I've been in the Highlands, man and boy, for the best part of a week. So I've had time to acquire the Highland gift of second sight. And my mental gaze pierces the foggy future and lets me prophesy with positive assurance that we're going to have a wonderful day together at the fair. Can I buy you a ribbon or a 'fairing' or whatever it is that story-book Scottish swains buy for the girls they take to fairs? There's a song—"

> " 'He promised to buy me a bonnie blue ribbon
> To tie up my bonnie brown hair!' "

sang Kathleen to a ripply laughter of accompaniment on the yellowed keys. "That was the song you were thinking of, wasn't it? And I shall insist on a whole bag of gilded ginger-nuts, too, and a whole jug of ginger-beer, and a turn at the cocoanut-shy and a visit to the raree show, besides. Are you sure you can afford all those wild luxuries? I warn you I shall make you spend almost a shilling on me before the day is over."

"We'll be reckless spendthrifts," he promised, as portentously solemn as she, "even if it costs TWO whole shillings and if I have to swim back to the States for lack of passage money. This is going to be a party that time can date from."

"You *do* know how to play!" she laughed, delightedly. "Uncle says Americans are so busy making money that they never learn how to play. He says he read so. It isn't true. Or did you learn to play after you stopped having to make money? Or isn't that any of my business, and is it a rude thing to ask?"

"Nothing's rude for a playfellow to ask," he decreed. "I only wish I had known about the fair, in time to get a Merry Villager costume and to learn the right steps for the Dance Around the Maypole. I suppose they *do* dance around the Maypole, outside of operas and story books."

"Not in good Presbyterian Inverness-shire!" she rebuked him. "But the merry-go-rounds are almost as nice. And I'll insist on a merry-go-round ride. Perhaps on two."

"More godless expense!" he groaned. "Another tuppence, I suppose, at the very least. I'll come out of that fair, flat broke. . . . Sing to me."

It was almost midnight when at last he went to his room, after hours of desultorily happy talk, interspersed here and there with snatches of olden Hieland airs and of improvisations that Kathleen's idly wandering fingers evoked from the yellowing keys of the half-voiceless antique piano.

Before they parted for the night Garth and she had arranged to spend the next day on the furthermost moorcrests, overlooking Moray Firth, and to tramp as far as the tree-grown battleground slope of Culloden, to eat their luncheon sandwiches among the scattered cairn stones of the slain clansmen.

They breakfasted early, he and she, alone at the table; for the Macbeath had gone out before sunrise, so the butler told Kathleen, and had left no word as to when he might return.

Yet as they were about to set forth on their day's tramp, and as Kathleen had departed to the pantry to supervise the packing of their luncheon, Roy saw the gaunt black figure of his host striding up the winding road from the village below. Garth went out into the courtyard to greet him, hoping devoutly that a night's reflection had not altered the chief's half-determination to sell Stirling.

To his relief, Macbeath gave him an almost cordial nod as they met. Then the chief drew him out of earshot of the open doors of the hall and said, rapidly:

"Mr. Garth, I have been turning over in my mind the matter you broached last night. I have decided to accept your offer. I do not pretend I am glad to do this. But ten thousand dollars is too much money for a poor man like myself to keep on four legs."

Roy sought to assume a poker face and to quiet his voice as he said, almost indifferently:

"Thanks. I'll be glad to have him. He is a fine dog."

"So I have suspected," dryly assented the Laird. "I am honored that you endorse my humble judgment of him. Yes, I will sell him to you. As Romeo's Apothecary says, 'My poverty and not my will consents.' But there are conditions."

He paused. Roy's heart abated a jot of its exultant beating, and he fell on guard again.

"Yes?" he asked, cautiously.

"You are paying me ten thousand dollars—roughly two thousand guineas," said Macbeath, "to gratify a mere millionaire whim. While I may have my own opinion of a man who will throw away that enormous sum upon a whim and upon a dog, yet I would be more foolish than he if I did not profit by it. (You will note I am observing your dictum that nothing can be gained by haggling, so I accept the price as it stands. Moreover, I am a chief, not a chafferer.)

"Therefore I will make out a formal bill of sale and a certified pedigree and a receipt; and I will turn them over to you along with Stirling, in exchange for the certified Bank of England checks which you agreed to pay me. Naturally, I am aware that ten thousand dollars is more money than two thousand pounds," he added craftily. "About fifty-nine pounds more, if I figure it aright. So you can give me your personal check, if you will, for the difference."

"Gladly," answered Roy. "And if that is the 'condition' you spoke of—"

"It is only one of them," corrected Macbeath. "I used the word in its plural, as belike you'll have noted. Here is the situation: While you and I may be educated beyond silly superstitions, yet my clansmen are not. I told you the 'Laird's Luck' legend, I think—that my house's fortune and safety rest on my having a collie of the Harailt line here with me. My people believe in that as you believe in the solar system. If it be known that I have parted voluntarily with my 'Luck,' the story will fly as fast over the hills hereabout as ever did the signal of the Fiery Cross in the old rallying days. It will smash my prestige, for which I care little. But also it will smash the remnants of my credit; for which I care much, as I still wish to gratify my morbid cravings to eat food and to wear clothing."

"Then—?"

"Then none of my clansmen—not even my niece, Mr. Garth, not even my niece—is to know I have parted with Stirling. My head shepherd, Comyn, alone of the whole kittle-kattle lot, can be trusted to the death, to keep any secret of mine. Not that Comyn loves me o'er much, but because I can send him to the gallows, at will, for a trifling murder I saw him commit, of a fellow-shepherd, some eight years agone.

"I shall order Comyn, tomorrow morning, with much publicity, to take Stirling with him to Cateran Mountain with the sheep he is driving there, to give him a week of herding. I do it every year, to keep the dog in mind of his puppy lessons at shepherd work. Comyn will have him crated and ready for transporting at the Ferrol railroad station, tomorrow night, in time for the nine-o'clock Edinburgh express.

"You will meet him there and travel south with him. You may telegraph at once to Southampton to reserve passage for yourself and the dog on the next outbound steamship. I think one will sail in about two days. I shall see that you get a telegram today calling you back at once to your own counting-house or office in America. The telegraph clerk at Ferrol is of my clan. He will arrange it for me. (By the way, if you will write your telegram to the steamship offices I will have it carried across to Ferrol this morning.) Neither my niece nor any other is to know you have the dog. I will have the bill of sale and the other transfer papers ready for you by this evening. Is that satisfactory? It will *have* to be satisfactory. So pray say Yes."

Garth conquered a crazy impulse to do a war dance on the courtyard's broken stone flagging.

Then Kathleen came out of the dark hall and stood framed on the threshold, with the flood of morning sunlight bathing her supple body and her bronzed face.

Somehow the mad impulse of joy deserted Roy. No longer had he any desire to let off steam by capering about.

There was no longer any steam to let off. Garth was about to take home the super-dog on whose possession his worldly future hung. But also he was leaving behind him this Scots lass. Angrily he asked himself what that could matter to him, when he was going back to fortune and to the girl he adored. He found no answer to the question. But neither did he find a return of his exultation.

He followed Macbeath to the study. There he scribbled a telegram to a steamship agency, bespeaking a cabin for himself on the next west-bound ship from Southampton—an easy thing to engage, at this non-tourist season—and accommodations in the boat's kennel room for the dog he was bringing along.

Next he sent in code a wire to Rufus G. Belden; a message which, decoded, ran:

"Have bought Stirling for ten thousand dollars. Am returning with him on the first available boat. Hallelujah! Incidentally, hip-Hosanna!"

The hallelujah and hosanna were perfunctory; and were for Belden's benefit, not for his own. For himself, Roy was able to concentrate only on the fact that as soon as these messages should be written he would be at liberty to spend a whole God-given day on the upland moors with Kathleen Macbeath.

CHAPTER NINE

———

THE London express was thudding southward. Scotland lay behind; so did the north country of England. The train was chirring through the smutty Midlands, bournes of smoky cities and smoky skies and grimed sheep and smudged faces.

In a goods van, snug in a big woven hamper, was the collie. In a first-class smoking compartment sat Roy Garth, sucking at a black old pipe, his mind lagging far behind the smooth-rushing express and centering unwillingly upon an upraised and bronzed face with level chin and honest brown eyes—a face as full of sweet and unafraid friendliness as a child's. His hands still answered to the lingering good-by grip of cool and strong little fingers.

Then through his sweet-sad reverie a troubling thought edged its way into Garth's mind—a thought that would not be banished and which obtruded more and more painfully as the hours went on.

Perhaps his few days in the depths of the Old World Highlands had inoculated him with a grain of the immemorial Highland faculty for premonitions. At all events, he was becoming more and more obsessed by the illogical notion that this entire transaction had been carried through too easily.

There was something suspicious about the effortless ease with which he had achieved his goal. He had gone to the castle—his one slight difficulty had been in gaining ingress there—he had made his offer; the offer had been accepted almost without demur.

Here he was, in incredibly short time, starting for home with the dog, his certified checks in Macbeath's worn wallet, and Stirling's "papers" safe in his own small handbag; the bag wherewith he had hammered his way through Ulrich's associates on the tree-strewn hillside beyond Midwestburg.

Jamie Mackellar had warned him of countless possible perils and setbacks. His own forebodings had fraught the mission with danger and with need for physical courage and strength, as well as for wit. Yet he had accomplished it all with little more of difficulty and less of time than would be involved in the buying of a new Poole greatcoat.

It did not make sense. It was too easy. Something was wrong, somewhere. In vain he pooh-poohed his grumbling premonitions. They would not quiet down and leave him in peace.

A wire received at Edinburgh had borne out further the facility of the whole thing by assuring him of a stateroom on a boat that was due to sail from Southampton in little more than six hours after his express was due in

London. In another day, he told himself, there would be blue water between him and Great Britain, and he and Stirling would be on the last lap of their journey to America.

When he reached Southampton his brooding worry had cast about until it found something definite to fasten on. He had had no trouble in buying Stirling. But suppose Stirling had been harmed in some way during the long train ride or in one of the several changes of cars!

Improbable as this chance appeared, he resolved to banish it once and for all. He went along the line of traveling coaches until he reached the goods vans. Their contents had just been unloaded. Porters were busy with them.

Readily Garth identified the woven hamper with its flaring red label of "Live Dog," and with his own name and Stirling's destination written on its tags. He stood beside it and chirped to the collie. There was no responsive sound or motion from within the hamper.

Troubled, Roy unlocked the crate and opened its top a few inches, peering in. There, by the uncertain light, he saw the collie, standing upright and returning the American's querying look.

Yes, the dog was not only alive, but on his feet. His feed trough was empty, which had been so full at starting. The collie then was not even sick. He had been able to eat. Roy saw his own foolish fears had been in vain.

Relieved, he put his hand in through the narrow slit at the hamper top, at the same time calling Stirling by name.

He withdrew his hand from the hamper much faster than he had inserted it. Across the wrist was a graze from which blood began to ooze.

The dog had slashed viciously at him. Only the instinctive quickness wherewith Roy had yanked away his hand had saved him from an ugly wound.

Garth blinked in utter amazement. Stirling had of his own accord declared friendship with him. When a high-quality collie does that, he is not likely to snap or slash at his human friend; especially when he recognizes the latter's voice and scent.

Roy looked again into the slightly opened hamper. The collie crouched, growling up at him. Again Garth spoke his name; talking soothingly to him, in the possibility that the long and unaccustomed journey had frayed Stirling's high-strung nerves.

By way of response the dog gave a sudden upward spring, hurling himself against the top of the hamper. So unexpected was the jump that Garth was taken by surprise and had no time to clamp shut the wicker top.

The lid smote Roy across the face as it banged upward. Out catapulted the big red-gold collie. As the dog leaped for freedom, Garth seized his fast-flying body by the ruff. Snarling, the dog whirled in air and tore at the imprisoning hand.

But Garth had had the deftness to catch him by the back of the neck, in front of the shoulders, and to hold the writhing seventy-pound body at arm's-length. Snarl and snap and wriggle as the crazed dog might, he could not close his ravening jaws on any part of the man's anatomy.

Roy was astounded at the once-friendly collie's ferocity. His long and intimate study of dog nature told him such a change was impossible. Yet it was happening. Soothingly, then sternly, he spoke to the fierce brute; but to no avail at all.

Then, subconsciously, something registered in his amazed brain; something which his sensitive fingers transmitted to his mind.

Two of his finger tips were in contact with a transverse ridge, far under the mattress of neck fur—a ridge that felt like a cord or thick hempen string, but which ran in zigzag fashion impossible to taut cord. Unquestionably the ridge was the weal of a long-healed scar that had cut deep into the flesh of neck and shoulder; perhaps a cut left by barbed wire as the dog had wriggled through a fence.

At all events, the scar must have been there a long time. There had been no such seam on Stirling's neck when Garth's practiced fingers had "gone over" every inch of the glorious collie's conformation, in dog-show-judge style, at Macbeath Castle.

Right carefully Roy had examined Stirling for malformations or for skin blemishes. He could take oath there was no such disfiguring ridged scar on the dog's neck and shoulder, beneath his shaggy mane.

Instinctively now, as the thought took hold on him, his grip tightened on this struggling collie's ruff, till the dog cried out in pain at the convulsive clutch. Garth slackened his hold, but still held the animal securely, staring at him in the dim twilight.

At the railroad station in Ferrol, when Comyn had turned over to him the beast in the crate, Garth had peeped in between the meshes of the wicker hamper and, by the flickering glimmer of the station's lamps, he had seen a huge red-gold collie of Stirling's appearance. The glimpse had satisfied him.

Now, disregarding the collie's struggles, Roy dragged him from the half-obscurity of the platform to the nearest electric light. Beneath the powerful white glare he surveyed his purchase.

At first glance this was Stirling, not only in color but in general aspect. A casual outsider, having seen Stirling only once or twice, might well have mistaken the high-quality collie twisting and snapping under the light-flare for the Macbeath super-dog.

But Roy Garth was anything but a mere casual observer. Not only had he made a fad of collies from earliest boyhood, but he had studied every line and every angle and every expression of Stirling, from a dozen viewpoints, during the past few days. To an expert, two outwardly similar collies are as much unlike in looks as are two humans of the same general height and coloring.

No, this dog was not Stirling. A minute's keen inspection proved that to Garth, past all doubt. This was a fine upstanding show-collie, and might well make his mark in any ordinary dog show. In color of coat and in general expression and contour he was much like the Macbeath dog—"The Luck of the Laird."

It was possible they were related to one another on the dam's side. For there was a strong family resemblance. But this collie was to Stirling what a first-rate light-opera tenor's voice would have been to Caruso's; what a clever young landscape painter's art would have been to Corot's; what a crack amateur heavyweight's prowess would be to the champion's.

This was not the collie which Roy Garth had bought —the collie whose "papers" he was hoarding in his handbag.

He had been cheated; even as Isaac was cheated by the pseudo-Esau whom Jacob impersonated, and as Jacob in turn was cheated by the tender-eyed Leah when he deemed her to be the fairer Rachel for whom he had slaved seven dreary years.

Now Garth understood, with sickening vividness, why the chief's first rage at the offer had merged into suavity; and why he had consented so willingly to sell Stirling as soon as he had been able to go out into the hills, next morning, and assure himself that he could still procure the dog whose outward likeness to Stirling was so remarkable.

Macbeath and his crooked head shepherd had done the rest. It had been a ludicrously easy task to dupe the American blockhead. Presumably Roy would not have gotten a good look at the substituted collie until he and the dog should be well out on the ocean, too late to come back and complain, even if the Yankee had the wit to discover the deception.

It must have seemed a safe trick to play—a trick whereby the Macbeath sold for ten thousand dollars a collie worth perhaps three hundred dollars at most. He could not have guessed that Garth would take another peep at the safely crated dog before sailing; or that doing so, he could detect the difference.

Yes, the wily old Highlander had played almost safe. But for an off-chance and for his own supposedly foolish worrying, Roy would have boarded the ship without a suspicion that he had been tricked.

Small wonder that Macbeath had vowed him to secrecy! Small wonder he had insisted, especially, that Kathleen know nothing of the deal!

Kathleen!

Back to Garth's memory rushed the vision of the Highland girl. Momentarily it swept away every other thought.

Then she in turn was brushed aside by the blackly raging anger which possessed him—anger at the dishonest old Laird and tenfold hotter wrath at his own stupid gullibility.

He dragged the dog to the crate and ordered a passing porter to carry the hamper to the near-by railway station. There, addressing a card, he shipped the collie back to Macbeath.

Without so much as stopping to cancel his passage on the steamship, Garth hired a motor car to take him and his luggage back to London, ahead of the first London-bound train.

Arriving in the metropolis—after a two-puncture delay—he found he had missed the outbound Edinburgh express by a matter of minutes. Fumingly he resigned himself to wait in London until morning. But in the morning his taxi collided with a bus on the way to the station. Followed an interminable waste of time while a helmeted and chin-strapped policeman jotted down in a notebook with precise slowness every fact that could or could not bear upon the mishap.

Garth reached the station a minute late for his train; and was forced to wait until eight o'clock that evening for the northbound express he wanted.

The needless delay added the traditional last straw to the American's loss of self-control. He raged impotently, and made futile plan after futile plan for the forcible capture of Stirling and for the punishment of the Laird.

Keenest of all ranked the memory of the jubilantly cocksure hallelujah telegram he had sent to Rufus G. Belden. Even now at Beldencroft, Rufus G. and Jamie Mackellar must be rejoicing. Phyllis must be thrillingly proud of his exploit, despite her mockery of the whole expedition. Then, unless in the next day or two he could accomplish the impossible, he must go home and face them all with news of his dire failure!

The thought stung him to renewed fury of resolve to recapture Stirling or to leave his own bones among the Inverness-shire moors. He had bought the collie, fairly and with good cash, at the price agreed upon. He had paid for him. He held Macbeath's legal receipt and bill of sale. The law would back him up in any endeavor to regain his own property.

Then he recalled that in this wild corner of the Highlands, Macbeath himself was the law and was slavishly obeyed by a thousand loyal clansmen. A hundred of them, doubtless, would be willing to perjure themselves in his behalf, saying the substituted dog was Stirling. The real Stirling could be hidden safely from sight while the perfunctory search of the police should go on.

No, the law could not help Garth. He knew that he and he alone could hope to get the dog. Against him would be all the wile and power of the chief. Roy was not optimistic over his own chances of success. But, as ever, the desperateness of the forlorn hope made him the more eager.

Night had fallen when Roy debarked from the Highlands train at Ferrol, nearly twenty-four hours later; after another maddening series of petty delays and of missed connections. There was still seven miles to travel, by bad roads, to Thross. Garth sought out the station master and asked for the one livery automobile which Ferrol possessed.

Apologetically he was told that it had been chartered, three hours earlier, to take to the castle the valet and the luggage of a new-arrived guest of the Laird's. The station master added the information:

"Mebbe ye'll be kenning him, sir; him being a foreigner like yersel'. 'Tis the master, not the valet, I mean. He'll be a Mr. Brant Ulrich, the master will, so his valet was a-tellin' me. From the States he is. He'll have come to castle, yester mornin', he did. The valet he don't come till this afternoon."

Garth gaped foolishly at the speaker. From the first, he had been looking for Brant Ulrich to appear in quest of the dog, to outbid Roy or to discredit him. But he had not realized Brant could have the wit to take his own time and to secure beforehand such difficult letters of introduction or other and more expensively forceful credentials from Edinburgh or London, as might coerce Macbeath into accepting him as an honored house guest.

Ulrich was on the ground—Ulrich with his boundless money and his tremendous influence and his tigerish guile. Ulrich was there, at the castle. He had Macbeath's ear. He could play successfully on the chief's piteous need for ready cash, to buy the real Stirling. He would be far too cunning—and Macbeath would recognize the fact—to be duped as Garth had been, by a substitute.

Roy's already impossible errand suddenly became tenfold more impossible. And this very impossibility woke his determination to new heat.

He checked his luggage in the station parcel room and set forth afoot over the seven miles of hill and dale toward Thross.

In an hour and a half he was climbing the winding castle rock. He tugged at the rusty bell pull, outside the gates. Presently the apelike porter appeared, grumbling and muttering. He stared in wide-mouthed astonishment at the returned Yankee guest whom he supposed to be halfway across the Atlantic by this time.

"I wish to see the Laird, at once," said Roy, with no further greeting.

Memories of the generous farewell tip bestowed by the young American made the porter almost civil.

"He'll be in the study with his new friend, sir," said he. "O'er their *uisge* and their coffee like. The dinner is ate, but I could get ye a mickle o' food and a basin o' brose, gin ye be peckish. I—"

"No," interrupted Roy, moving past him. "I wish to see the Laird. I won't wait to be announced. I know my way."

He crossed the flagged and vaulted hall toward the passage leading to the chief's study. Faintly, as he went, he could hear Kathleen's piano from the niche room on the hall's other side. But he steeled his heart to the musically whispering appeal, and kept on.

CHAPTER TEN

———

THE study door was ajar. Garth went in without knocking, and closed it behind him. Two men sat at the hearth, a bottle-and-glass-littered tabouret between them. Facing Roy, was Brant Ulrich, sleekly powerful and lazy as a Bengal tiger. He was smiling courteously at something the Laird was telling him, and in one hand he toyed with a liqueur glass.

The Macbeath was in full Highland regalia. His shoulder was to the door and to the man who had entered.

"Yes," the Laird was saying, "the flower of the clans was in the front line of battle, there, just at the end of the slope, to the south of Culloden Ridge. On the right, as I told you, were the Murrays—and by the way, those same Murrays used to take a more than neighborly interest in my own ancestors' cattle, from time to time—when my ancestors weren't taking the same neighborly interest in theirs. (You know, most of our heroic Highland clans, in those days, spent their spare time in robbing any neighbor it was safe to rob. They had to keep from starving, I suppose, though for the life of me I can't see why.) Well, next to the Murrays stood the Camerons—with Cameron of Lochiel at their head, the dour old freebooter! The center was held by the MacIntoshes and the Frasers and the MacLeans of Lochbuy, and the Farquharsons and the Stuarts of Appin and the—"

Noting the shift of his guest's gaze as it focused in amused surprise on the doorway, Macbeath turned and saw Garth. For a flicker of time the gaunt old scoundrel blinked, nonplused. Instantly, however, his slant black brows settled shieldingly over the coal-black eyes and his seamed face expressed only chill interest in the unexpected arrival.

"I did not hear you announced, Mr. Garth," he said, stiffly. "Perhaps in America it is your custom to give your hosts a joyous surprise by sneaking into their houses like a—"

"Like a freebooter?" suggested Roy, steadying his voice. "I have heard you boast that your own ancestors were thieves. Such traits seem to be hereditary. You have stolen from me a dog I bought from you and for which I hold your receipt. I have come back for him."

Ulrich jumped up indignantly, at the black insult to his host. But Macbeath sat back in his rickety hearth chair, smilingly imperturbable.

"In the good old days," purred the Laird huskily, "when a low fellow wished ingress to a noble's castle, he collected to him other low fellows; and they assailed the walls. Thus, either as conqueror or as prisoner, he stood a bright chance of standing face to face with the man he sought. Now, apparently, he bribes servants, and thus he crawls in, unnoticed. I merely comment on it, in passing. You were speaking of a dog, I believe? Do you refer to the collie you admired while you gave my poor house the undeserved and undesired honor of visiting it?"

"I do," said Garth, trying to keep cool. "I refer to the dog I bought and paid for and whose papers I hold—papers signed by yourself. You substituted a lesser collie for him, and you palmed this other dog off on me. I shipped the second dog back to you. He ought to be here by tomorrow. Now I have come for Stirling—for my own dog. Please give him to me."

Macbeath smiled apologetically at Brant Ulrich, as if entreating his leniency for the erratic stranger. In the look the two men exchanged Garth read, as in a flash of inspiration, that they had already come to a full understanding. The pair were so much alike in character and temperament that only the shortest time must have been needed to place them in total accord with each other.

Brant unquestionably had been told of the trick played on Garth; and equally certainly had made an offer of his own for Stirling, presumably a much higher and more satisfactory bid than Garth's. Whether or not Macbeath meant to play fair with this new and craftier guest, was no concern of Roy's. But Garth could see the two were allies. That was the only phase of their mutual situation which interested him.

"Mr. Ulrich," said Macbeath, smoothly, "I crave your indulgence for this fellow-countryman of yours. He is either drunk or insane. In either case I don't wish him here."

He finished his speech by rising and pulling the tapestried bellrope that dangled beside the hearth.

"I am giving you a chance to make good," declared Garth, going up to the Laird. "Will you give Stirling to me, of your own will, or must I apply to the police?"

"I have sold the collie to you, Mr. Garth," answered Macbeath, "as your own bill of sale and receipt and pedigree will prove. You took him to Southampton with you. You say you are shipping him back to me. Very good. By all means take the case to the police. I shall be glad to supply innumerable witnesses to prove he is the dog you bought. I repeat, you are either drunk—"

"Suborn a hundred of your clansmen to swear what you tell them to," flashed Garth. "*I* shall call just one witness. And that one witness's square testimony will outweigh all their lies, put together, in any court of law. I shall call on Miss Kathleen Macbeath to say in court, under oath, whether or not the dog you palmed off on me is Stirling."

Macbeath's face went wooden stiff. Garth could see his shot had found its mark.

"You will please have the decency not to take my niece's clean name on your drunken lips, Mr. Garth," rebuked Macbeath, sternly, though his voice had lost a shade of its dryly rasping calmness. "We need not bring her into this sordid squabble. I wish you to leave this house. Take your case to the police, by all means. Take it to the devil, for all I care. Only get out of here."

"I stay here," asserted Roy, stoutly, "until I can get satis—"

"Oh," grunted Macbeath as the butler answered belatedly his master's repeated ringing, "you're here at last. I want this man thrown out. Get help and do it. Waste no time."

Wondering, the butler withdrew. Brant Ulrich spoke for the first time.

"I shall be happy to toss this sot out for you," he told Macbeath, lazily flexing his giant muscles, "if the job is not in your servants' line."

"I'm glad you've come in range, Ulrich," mocked Roy. "I am a stickler for etiquette, of a sort. So I didn't like to speak to you unless you spoke first. You see, I wasn't quite sure how you'd feel toward me after I bashed your face in with my handbag, that night you and your little comrades tried to send me to the hospital, back at Midwestburg. I wasn't certain just how you would take it or take the ducking your henchman got when his motorcycle went into the creek. It was quite a pleasant two minutes—for me. But I'm afraid the pleasure was all mine. Now that you've broken the ice, by your cordial offer to throw me out, the out-throwing festivities can begin at once, if you like. As they may be lengthy, not to say rough, I suggest you start in without waiting any longer."

The two Americans were facing each other, tense, alert, savage. So do two fighting dogs stand for a brief moment, searching warily a death grip before they fling themselves into battle.

The tension was broken by the reappearance of the butler. At his heels shambled the apelike porter, incredibly powerful in his grotesque awkwardness.

"I needn't trouble you, Mr. Ulrich," said Macbeath. "My fellows here can do the work quite satisfactorily. There is no need in your soiling your hands. We—"

The Laird broke off abruptly, even as he turned to signal his servants to take hold of Garth.

The noise of voices had crossed the hall and to the niche room beyond, penetrating through the soft-played music. Drawn by the angry sound, Kathleen stood in the doorway.

"Miss Macbeath!" cried Garth, stepping eagerly toward her.

With quickness surprising in so old a man, the chief intervened his own gaunt body between them, even as a light of joyous welcome sprang into the girl's dark eyes at sight of Roy.

"You will please leave the room, Kathleen," ordered Macbeath, speaking gently but with infinite authority. "This man has come back here, offensively drunk, and he has insulted us all. It is not a scene for you to—"

"But, uncle," she pleaded, aghast, even as her worried eyes scanned Roy's excitedly flushed face for confirmation or denial of the charge, "he—"

"He lies, Miss Macbeath!" exclaimed Roy, beside himself, his voice thick and shaken. "He has—"

"You will leave the room," repeated the chief, his black eyes beginning to smolder as they held Kathleen's bewilderedly appealing gaze in half-hypnotic grip. "You will leave the room at once, Kathleen. *At once!*"

Schooled to lifelong obedience of her elders and to ancestral obedience to the chief of her clan, the girl turned slowly and made her way from the room. Garth called her name eagerly and made as if to go to her. The butler and the porter, in the same instant, had him by the arms.

Macbeath closed and locked the heavy door behind his niece, even as Roy wrenched free from the dual grasp. Lightly Garth sprang back, as again the two servants came at him. The maneuver brought him within arm's-length of Brant Ulrich.

Brant had moved to the fireplace as Kathleen came in; and had stood there, taking no part in the proceedings.

Roy leaped back, braced to meet the assault of the grimly oncoming servants. Ulrich reached out to the table and picked up the heavy silver-covered liqueur bottle that Roy had mistaken for a weapon a few nights earlier when he had seen it in the butler's hand in the half-light of the passageway.

And now the bottle justified itself as a weapon. With a snake-swift drive of his mighty arm Ulrich brought down the silver-enforced glass container upon the crown of Garth's head. He struck, unseen, from behind, and with all his trained athletic force.

The thick glass was splintered into a hundred fragments. The strong silver sheathing buckled and crumpled.

Roy Garth's knees turned to tallow. He slumped, spinelessly, and pitched forward on his face, at the Laird's feet.

"Well struck!" approved the Macbeath, glancing at the sprawled and bleeding Garth and then admiringly at his assailant. "Very commendably struck. I can find it in my heart to overlook the loss of the decanter given by Charles II to my ancestor, Clomnel Macbeath of Ferrol, for the sake of witnessing such a really pretty blow. But wasn't it wasted effort? My men could have done the work quite as thoroughly."

"No," denied Ulrich, nursing his chafed palm, as he eyed the two dumfounded menservants. "No, it was not a wasted effort. It was mighty necessary, if we're to do something that I'll suggest for your own safety as well as for my chance at getting the dog. I got the idea when he spoke of calling your niece as a witness. He mustn't be able to do that. It would wreck everything. If you'll send away your men, I'll explain. . . . Thanks."

Roy woke to pain-shot dizziness, to find himself lying in a pitch-dark place that smelled of onions. His head was one throbbing agony, and shooting pains ran all over his limp body.

Dumb and moveless he lay there, trying to piece together his scattered powers of thought. His brain began to clear. Bit by bit and then coherently he remembered what had happened, up to the time he sprang back to meet the attack of the porter and the swarthy butler. All after that was blank.

Ulrich's blow had been shrewdly delivered. But the ancient glass of the bottle was full of flaws. Also, Garth had chanced to move his head an inch or so to one side as he stepped backward within reach of the blow. The result had been a deflection from the straight line and an unduly easy collapse of the bottle.

A clean knockout had been scored and the victim had been rendered unconscious for many minutes thereafter. Yet the skull was intact and a tough constitution was combining with Youth to cast off the paralyzing effects of the shock.

At last Roy sought to lift an exploratory hand to his throbbing head. It was then he discovered he was neatly bound, wrists and ankles, by rawhide thongs of much strength. The knowledge drove away the last of the shock-mists from his brain. He had supposed that there had been a scrimmage in which he had been struck senseless and that then he had been pitched ignominiously out of the castle. But it seemed he was a prisoner.

His eyes were accustoming themselves to the dim light. An oblong of lighter color appeared at one side of the dark. This he took to be a doorway, leading out into the open.

Then the dimness was split, briefly, by a stab of reddish light that made him squint.

In the doorway sat a huge-shouldered man, a gun across his knees. He was in the act of lighting his pipe.

The flare of the match cast a faint glow through Garth's prison, in the moment before it was blown out. Roy saw he was lying on a heap of bags in a small stone storehouse, one of the several outbuildings which strewed the farther end of the castle's shabby courtyard. He could make out the dim bulk of the turret between him and the sky. Close at his side were a deep pannikin of water and a loaf of oatcake, by way of provision.

He recognized his guard as the apelike porter from whose gorilla grip he had wrenched himself free earlier in the evening. Summoning his voice from somewhere in the depths of him by a great effort, Garth asked:

"What's the idea of the melodramatic trussing up? Why not put me in the turret, so I can sing a *Miserere* through the bars, instead of making me inhale onions in a shack like this?"

The porter turned about in leisurely fashion and favored the captive with a monstrous sour glare.

"The turret's na' for a maudit wastrel like yersel'!" he growled. "Root-shed be guid enow for ye. Here ye be and here ye stop till Davy can win to Innoch and fetch constables to jail ye."

"Jail me?" repeated Garth. "Then this isn't a private Hieland feud, eh? What am I to be jailed for?"

As if repeating a hard-learned lesson, the porter replied:

" 'Tis weel kent ye're a monstrous desprit character. Ye trespassed into castle an' ye forced a winder and a braw strong door to git in yon."

"What's that?" demanded Roy, amazed.

"We be ready to show constable the busted winder and door and the bar ye used to break and enter," the porter assured him. "Then ye assaulted and battered the Laird himself, no less, wi' yer gret fists. Unprovoked it were, as we can tek oath on. Him an owd man, too, wha' greeted ye friendly-like. Mon, 'tis five years in quod that ye'll be gittin', nae less!" he ended virtuously.

Then, turning his back with elaborate scorn on the vile foreigner, the porter resumed his inspection of the outer night, puffing at his rank pipe and nursing the gun between his knees.

Garth's mind had scope no longer for remembering that his head ached and that he was sore all over. Clearly he saw the Macbeath's whole clever scheme, and as clearly did he see its perils to himself. The story would go—with fervently perjurous witnesses—Ulrich doubtless among them—that Garth had entered feloniously and by force the home of his recent host and then had launched a murderous attack on that host, an aged and harmless man—a laird, at that, and in a region where the jury would be Macbeath's own kinsfolk and his clansmen.

Apparently, Macbeath and Ulrich had had the supposedly homicidal intruder tied up and put under guard, to make a greater impression on the constables when they should arrive. Truly, Brant had made his crafty presence felt during his short stay in the Highlands!

For minutes Roy lay moveless, but with his mind arace. The rawhide thongs hurt his wrists and his ankles.

In boyhood, when he and his friends played "Apache" he had been tied up thus, once, and the rawhides had teased his ankles and wrists as now they did. What had he done then? He remembered he had gotten himself free, and that he had done it by using a trick he had read about in a Sunday-school library book's reminiscences of an Indian fighter. But what was the trick?

His pain-twisted face assumed a grin. At last he recalled the whole procedure.

Noiselessly he plunged his hands and wrists into the pannikin at his side, and held them there, the rawhide well under water. The restless gesture had not made the porter look back at him.

The thongs grew wetter and wetter, softer and softer, more and more pliant, as is ever the way of soaked leather, and especially true of rawhide. At last Garth began to manipulate his bound hands. By strength and by leverage he stretched the wet hide, even as it cut deeper into him at every effort.

Then one hand writhed free, leaving a copious tribute of barked wrist skin on the dangling thong. Garth reached into his hip pocket for his penknife to cut the ankle bonds. The knife was gone. The pocket was turned inside out.

Every pocket had been treated thus. But into one— the side pocket of his coat—had been stuffed his money and his watch and his pipe and tobacco pouch and match-safe—every possession but his knife.

This discovery startled Garth far more than had the

fact that he was a prisoner, bound and guarded. His captors had ransacked his clothes—even, as his exploring fingers told him, to slitting the linings of his coat and his waistcoat. Then, contemptuously, they had slung back into one pocket his valuables. Thus they had not been actuated by desire to steal these belongings, but had been in quest of something else. Of what?

With the question the answer flashed across him. He recalled the stiffening of the Laird's face when Garth had threatened to call Kathleen as a court witness in his behalf. That threat must have sunk deep into the old blackguard's nerves.

One thing alone could render the girl's testimony valueless.

If Macbeath could lay his hands on the bill of sale and on the signed receipt for Stirling and on the other transfer papers he had turned over to Roy, then Garth would have absolutely nothing but his own worthless word to prove that he had bought the dog. This the Macbeath could do; or he could alter the documents by substituting another collie's name for Stirling's, in case Garth should call on the railway officials to back his claim that he had carried a dog to Southampton.

They had been searching his senseless body for those papers, Macbeath and Ulrich. There could be no doubt of it.

With deep-breathed gratitude Garth rejoiced that he had not been able to find a car to bring him to Thross from the railway station at Ferrol this night. He had left behind him in the parcel room all his luggage, including the little handbag in which were Stirling's "papers" and a fat sheaf of express checks and his passport and other guard-worthy things.

The bag was safe in the station parcel room at Ferrol, along with Garth's heavier luggage, where neither Macbeath nor Ulrich could think of looking for it. They did not even know how he had come to Thross, or that his luggage might not be at any of fifty places along the route from Southampton; or indeed that he kept the transfer papers in the handbag.

On the natural supposition that the papers were in his pockets, they had searched him as thoroughly as ever was a war spy searched. And until they could find the transfer papers, the game was by no means in their own hands.

Garth had another flash of inspiration as he sat up silently and began to pick at the knots that bound his ankles: In all likelihood, this cock-and-bull story of felonious trespass and assault might have been staged for the sake of sending an emissary to him in jail, before the trial, with an offer to drop the case in return for the documents attesting Stirling's sale. With these papers out of Macbeath's possession and in Roy's, the final advantage must be with Garth.

"It's like the dear old melodramas," mused Roy, "where the hero and the villain struggle on the cliff for the mysterious papers. I'm too much of a dub to be a hero. Well, the other end of the sketch makes up for it with a double portion of villainy."

Under his deft fingers the clumsy ankle knots came

undone at last. Roy had worked the more feverishly for knowing what must happen if he should fail to undo the bonds. For wet rawhide, in drying shrinks appallingly. If he had not been able to free himself of the thongs, they would have begun soon to shrink through skin and flesh and clean to the bone.

Oddly gay at having loosed his leathern fetters and given himself once more a chance to fight his way out, he bent his energies to getting rid of his stout guard.

An imp of mischief danced into Garth's brain as, groping noiselessly among the pile of sacks and torn coats and rags which formed his bed on the flagged floor, his fingers closed on a voluminous canvas bag, rumpled and mildewed, but still stout, and with a tough drawstring about its opening.

"Yuss!" grunted the porter, breaking his own long and disapproving silence. "Yuss, ye'll ha' bruk into castle like a robber an' ye'll ha' laid sacreleejus hands o' murder an' pillage on an owd man—on the Laird hissel', no less. On the Lord's anointed, as a body micht a'most say. D'ye speir to—? *Wough-r-r-r-r!*"

A section of the sky, sharply scented with onions and mold, swooped down over the speaker's head and shoulders and over his simian arms. The gun clattered to the stone flooring of the threshold. The porter was staggering about, blind and helpless, the upper half of his body smotheringly encased in a canvas bag whose drawstring Garth knotted tightly about the victim's middle.

A shove sent the porter sprawling among the scattered rags.

CHAPTER ELEVEN

Roy walked out, closing the door softly behind him. Two minutes later the refugee had slipped through the unbarred castle gates and was running down the winding rocky path toward the snoring village of Thross. He did not slacken pace until he was well out on the moors, under the misty starlight and with the heather-tinged night wind strong in his hot face.

Then he paused for breath and to plan the next move. Behind him in the cup of the hills snuggled the unlighted village. Above it, atop its high-jutting fortress rock, the single ruined turret of the castle outlined itself, sinister and grim, against the night sky.

Somewhere between the castle and the nearest police-station town, constables were hurrying to arrest the supposed assailant of Macbeath. By tomorrow the whole countryside would know of the alleged crime and it might turn out to waylay the foreign desecrater of Highland hospitality.

But for the moment Roy Garth had the night to himself and a fair start on the hue-and-cry. He filled and lighted his pipe and sat down on a boulder to ease his racked head and to think.

He saw he had behaved like a rash fool in running headlong to the castle and demanding his dog. He had dashed head-on into a hornet's nest in forcing himself upon Macbeath who had cheated him and on Ulrich who hated him. Naturally, the combination had been too strong for him and infinitely too clever.

There was but one sane thing to do, now—to tramp back to Ferrol, get his handbag out of the station parcel room, carry its transfer papers to the nearest reputable lawyer, and place the case unreservedly in his hands.

Justice would be done in that way—clean Scottish justice, not Highland-laird justice. Any good lawyer in Edinburgh or even in Perth or Inverness, could force Macbeath to make restitution. If the Laird should persist in claiming he had given Garth the dog named in the bill of sale, Kathleen's straightforward testimony would convince the court.

Kathleen!

Garth had an almost startling mental vision of her as she had stood in the study doorway, beneath the bulging gray canvas ceiling, her honest level eyes aglint with joyous surprise at seeing him again. And then—then she had been forced to leave the room, believing him the noisily drunken intruder her uncle claimed him to be.

Roy got to his feet and set off across the moors toward Ferrol. False dawn was beginning to whiten the eastern sky. The wind was freshening. He must take a full hour and a half to get to Ferrol, even across country.

Then he must get his luggage from the parcel room at the station and catch the first train to Inverness or to some other city where he could learn the name and address of a reliable solicitor into whose hands he could confide his case. Time enough, after that, to write to Belden and explain what had happened—when the wheels of justice should be in motion to get back the collie for him.

Fast he walked, the false dawn ebbing and the true dawn deepening as he went. Bird after bird awakened and sent up to heaven its hymn of praise for the coming day. From the brightening sky dropped shrill lark-songs. Here and there a red deer lunged to its legs from a bed of gorse and floundered noisily off in panic flight from the approaching human.

Hares, some of them snow white, scuttled from under Garth's very feet. A half-score of grouse, from time to time, blundered whirringly skyward from the bracken. A mile above, more and more larks were singing their hearts out. On all sides the long-haired gray sheep looked up from their early meal to blink dully at the intruder.

Lambs—hundreds upon hundreds of them, newborn and white and awkwardly frisky—cantered amid the grazing flocks. Gulls were flying inland for their daily feast in the plow furrows. There was a smell of the far-off sea in the air as the dawn wind whipped the night mists to tatters. Ravens flapped gloomily from the woods. Rooks cawed in the treetops.

Morning was breaking as Roy Garth entered Ferrol's

huddle of narrowly winding streets and made his way to the station. He feared to find the railway buildings closed at so early an hour. But the main station was open and a crowd was standing about its door.

Garth elbowed his way past the curiously staring idlers and entered the building, moving toward the parcel room, to one side of the booking office. Here he saw several railway attendants and officials and two constables filling the tiny room with their excited bodies. The door was hanging crazily from one hinge.

It was a matter of minutes for Garth to get the attention of one of the constables and of another two minutes to convince the policeman that he held a receipt for suitcases and a handbag stored there the night before.

Then as the constable took down his name, Roy was told that the station master, arriving to begin his day's work a half-hour earlier, had found the station's front door jimmied open and the parcel-room door in like condition.

A dozen bags and suitcases and packages, left there for safekeeping had been stolen, among them Roy Garth's luggage.

Roy listened to the tale of the robbery with ears that heard little and heeded less. All he knew or cared about it was that his precious handbag was gone, the bag that contained not only his passport and all his reserve money, but the papers proving his ownership of Stirling.

Except for the clothes he stood in—sadly rumpled and muddy and bloodstained from last night's encounter—

he had not another garment left. Except for about forty dollars in British currency, loose in his pockets, he was penniless. He had no credentials of any kind.

He stood all but bare and broke, more than three thousand miles from home and friends and safety. Seven miles away, at Thross, the local police must already be on the search for him. Without his passport he was in far worse peril from them than before. Without the sheaf of documents that dealt with the sale of Stirling he had not one weapon wherewith to defend himself from the Macbeath's atrocious accusations.

He was cleaned out, helpless, alone.

This, then, was the end of his jubilant quest, the end of his brilliant diplomatic overseas mission, the end of his cocky hopes for promotion—the end of his chance to claim Phyllis!

To his own dumb astonishment, the prospective loss of Phyllis sickened and saddened him far less than did any of the other certainties of misfortune entailed by the theft of his bag.

Try as he would, he could not retrieve the olden glamour of fascination wherein she had enwrapped him. By some trick of brain he found his thoughts dwelling longest and most miserably on Kathleen Macbeath; and he was angrily astonished that this should be so.

He had known Kathleen so short a time! And now she must be remembering him with disgust as a half-crazy drunkard who had repaid her hospitality by bursting into the castle, intoxicated, and by becoming quarrelsomely offensive there. The thought was like vitriol on a raw wound.

Mechanically Roy plodded over to the Ferrol post office. There he wrote and dispatched a brief code cable to Belden, to the effect that he had been robbed, and asking that two thousand dollars be cabled him to the local post office's care.

With luck, he knew the money ought to be at Ferrol inside of a day. Its possession would help him out in the hiring of lawyers to defend him against Macbeath's charges, and would otherwise make life less unbearable in this fair land where he was broke and a fugitive.

The castle porter had said that constables had been sent for, from some town in the vicinity, to arrest Garth. The town was not Ferrol; though Roy could not remember what place it was, as the name had meant nothing to him. But assuredly word would be sent to the police from one town to another, along with a description of him. Were he to loiter about Ferrol until the answer should be received to his cable, he stood a strong chance of arrest.

Soon or late, of course, the arrest must come. But he did not want it to find him without money which might aid him in hiring the right kind of lawyer and in procuring such comforts as cash may bring to a man in jail.

He decided to go out upon the moors again, to lose himself in their folds and tumbles and ravines, and to remain hidden until there was time for the cabled money to reach Ferrol. Then he could go back and claim it and, if necessary, give himself up to the police.

He strolled unconcernedly out of town. As he went he noted an unwonted life and bustle and gayety in the street. No shops were opening, but many folk were abroad, and all in gala attire. Scattered through the array of bright dresses and hats and black Sunday suits, were tartans and kilts. Dozens of men wore, this day, the ancient Highland garb, in place of their customary somber clothes.

For an instant Garth wondered. Then he remembered what Kathleen had said about the Spring Holiday—this festival peculiar to Scotland alone, whereon the official arrival of spring is celebrated by everyone who can spare time or pence for the outing.

He recalled her eager suggestion that he and she attend together the annual Spring Holiday Fair on Curragh Green, between Thross and Ferrol, and that she had been childlikely disappointed when she found a message from home demanded his instant return to America, so that he could not take her to the festivities. He had been touched by the simplicity of the girl whose sheltered life made her look forward with such infantile eagerness to so cheaply garish an outing.

He left Ferrol well behind him now, walking aimlessly but fast, with no objective but to reach some spot among the moors isolated and sheltered enough to hide him for the bulk of the day. Climbing a long roll of steep incline, he looked down upon a barren wild; stretching bleakly away toward a far-off ravine where piles of black peat had been cut and stacked.

But the heath itself was too bare and dead for peat or

for anything but sparse wire grass. Here in the midst of the lush spring beauty of the moorland it stretched like a leprous sore on the laughing face of the landscape.

Roy stood for a moment, eying with scant favor the rock-strewn expanse.

Not even a tiny flower seemed able to sustain life on this waste of heath which seemed almost as though it had been scorched by some ancient fire.

Halfway down the creased bare slope was a hollowed cup of ground, surrounded by misshapen boulders. Here, if anywhere, mused Garth, a man might hope to hide in safety on this day when shepherds were merry-making and when holiday-seekers would be likely to choose cheerier spots for their picnics.

Down the slope he went, his heels dislodging pebbles and slipping on the greasy gray turf. He had reached the brink of the hollow and was rounding the first boulder that guarded it when he came to an abrupt standstill.

Here in this desolate and God-forgotten place some-one was sobbing.

From not ten feet away from him, on the far side of the boulder, came the sound—unrestrained heartbroken sobs as when a hopeless child cries.

Apparently at least one other besides Garth was out of tune with the holiday spirit of the morning. Instinctively Roy stepped forward to investigate. Again he paused. In the little hollow at his feet crouched a woman. Her face was buried in her hands. Her slenderly athletic body was shaken by weeping.

But Garth needed no glimpse of the hidden features to know who the weeper was. His heart told him, even before his eyes recognized details of Kathleen Macbeath's figure that had grown so familiar and so dear to him.

Another pebble rolled from under his braced foot and rattled down the incline. Kathleen started at the sound, looking guiltily about her and stanching her tears with an absurdly inadequate morsel of handkerchief.

Her big eyes widened as they met Garth's. An expression something akin to superstitious awe flashed over her tear-scored features. For an instant he and she faced each other, alone together in the hollow of the eternal hills, neither of them speaking or moving, their eyes embracing, their bodies aloof and tense.

It was Kathleen who broke the spell. Her face flushed deeply and a fire shimmered behind her swimming eyes.

"Will you please go away?" she said, frigidly, standing very straight, her hands behind her. "It is not much to ask that you leave me in peace."

"No," he made answer, scarce above a whisper. "It is not much to ask. But it is too much to grant. I have not done anything to make you look at me and speak to me as if I were something slimy. I am not going to leave you thinking that way about me. If you believe I broke into your uncle's castle last night and that I attacked him or that I was drunk or abusive, as they told you I was, then you are believing a lie. I can't prove it. But on my word as a man, it is a filthy lie. Perhaps that sounds melodramatic. I don't care how it sounds, as long as you believe me. And you've simply *got* to believe me, Kathleen!"

Again fell that hush of silence between them, and again their eyes held each other's. Roy had an odd feeling that the girl was reading the very soul of him in that interminably long look.

"You know I am telling the truth," he said at last.

Another moment of silence, while far above a lark's song died in the blue spring sky. Then:

"Yes," she said, as simply as a child. "I believe you."

He drew a long breath of utter relief.

"I believe you," she went on, "I don't know why, but I do. All at once, just now, something behind your eyes told me it was right to believe you. And I do more: I know now that Mr. Ulrich was not telling us the truth last night when he said you were one of the most expert swimmers in America. Uncle had been telling him how Stirling and I helped you out of Loch Thross when you fell in and when you couldn't swim a stroke. Mr. Ulrich laughed; and he said you had won silver cups for swimming and diving, and he said—it was abominable of him —he said you must have just pretended to be drowning so as to get acquainted with me and get asked to the castle. At first I almost believed that, too, but now I know better. *You* couldn't have done it—Roy. You *couldn't*."

Then it was that Roy Garth performed the most sublimely, if foolishly, heroic action of his whole career.

"I am throwing away your trust," he began lamely, "and I haven't even the right to tell you it means more to me than any of a million other treasures I could have. But when you—when you are looking at me like that, I—I feel as if I were in a holy place. And somehow I can't lie to you. That is crazy, I know. But—here goes!"

He braced himself as if to meet a football rush. Then, his voice grating like a file, he went on:

"I was not drunk last night, Kathleen. I did not lay a hand on your uncle or threaten to. I didn't break into your home. The porter let me in when I rang. But the—the other thing is true."

"What thing?" she asked, perplexed.

"It is true I faked that drowning. It is true I did it to get an invitation to the castle. There isn't any excuse, except—except that I didn't know you. Knowing you, I could no more lie to you than I could tell a lie in my prayers. Not that that is any excuse. There, you've got the real truth! And I'll leave you now if you wish. I suppose I deserve all the things you're thinking of me."

He made as though to move away.

"Wait!" she commanded. "Wait! It's all so impossible —so absurd! Do you mean to tell me you went through all that, just for the sake of being invited into a tumble-down castle that isn't even a tourist site? That would be the action of an imbecile or else of a clown. You are not either one. *Why* did you do it, Roy?"

Neither of them noticed that involuntarily they were calling each other by their first names—a thing that had not occurred to them to do before during their brief acquaintance.

"*Why* did you do it?" she repeated. "You must have had some tremendous motive."

"I wanted to buy Stirling," he replied. "That sounds crazy or clownlike, too, I suppose. But it is true. I had heard about him in America. Jamie Mackellar saw him here, last year, and he said Stirling is the greatest collie alive. I crossed the ocean to buy him. I knew it might be hard to do, because I had heard that you people all believe in the legend about his being a sort of—of mascot —for your house. So I wanted to meet your uncle as a guest, if I could, and find a way then to bring up the subject. I—"

"Stirling?" she repeated, puzzled. "You mean Glamis. Comyn's head collie, Glamis. That is the dog you bought. Uncle said so. Not Stirling. No money could buy Stirling."

"Glamis is the dog I *got*," assented Garth, "though I didn't know his name till now. But I came here to buy Stirling. And I *did* buy Stirling. For ten thousand dollars. Your uncle sold him willingly enough. I see why, now. I saw why as soon as I found it was Glamis I had in the hamper. In my own country we'd call that a dirty deal. I played fair with Macbeath. I was honest with him. And he—"

The perplexity in her big eyes gave place to hot indignation. Fiercely she broke in on his miserable explanation:

"You 'played fair' with my uncle? Played *fair!* You American multimillionaires call it 'playing fair' when you come to Europe and find us so cruelly pinched for money that we have no choice but to accept the tons of banknotes you offer us for the things our ancestors won for us with their lives and with their fortunes, and that we prize as hallowed? You take advantage of our honorable poverty and of our longing for enough money to make life less harsh for those we love; so you drive shrewd Yankee bargains with our stark need.

"In return for our art treasures and the other things that are our lives' holy traditions, you toss us enough cash to keep us a little longer from starving. You tempt us beyond our strength and you play on our hunger. It is like Monte Cristo's offering to sell the starving banker a slice of bread for ten thousand francs.

"And you call it 'playing fair,' do you? And you wonder why hungry Europe does not love money-squandering Yankeedom! Would you love the man who came to you in your need and offered to ease your distress in return for the treasures that are dearest to you? Would you? Is it pleasant to think that our sacred heirlooms are being pawed over and gloated over and bragged over by millionaire vulgarians? 'Playing fair!' Your ideas of sportsmanship seem to be—"

"On a par with your uncle's?" supplemented Roy, as angry as she. "Not quite. The vulgar Yankee millionaires, as you so courteously call us, give full value for all they buy. (And please remember they couldn't buy anything at all from you people, if it wasn't for sale. There's that to think of.) We give full value, we vulgarians. We pay in honest cash.

"Europeans know, better than we, how often they

foist fake art treasures on us, instead of the real ones we pay for. Every few months the papers expose some such fraud. I paid your uncle ten thousand dollars for Stirling. He gave me a bill of sale and a transfer for him. Then he palmed off on me a dog that isn't worth one-thirtieth of ten thousand dollars. Yet you sneer at *our* sportsmanship!"

"I can't believe my uncle did any such abominable thing!" she declared. "You must have misunderstood him. And he would no sooner sell Stirling than—than—"

"I see now he wouldn't," agreed Roy, dryly. "But he took the price for him and he gave me the receipt, with Stirling's name on it. By the way, let me set you straight on one thing: You called me a multimillionaire vulgarian. The last part of it probably was true enough. I can't prove I'm not a vulgarian. But as for being a multi-millionaire—well, let me dazzle you with a full list of my wealth at the present minute. I—"

"I am not interested, I'm afraid," she began, "in—"

"On my oath," he went on, unheeding, "my worldly wealth consists of these badly mussed clothes I'm wearing, and this gold watch of doubtful pawnableness, and something under forty dollars in actual cash. That is the financial status of this particular vulgar Yankee multi-millionaire. No, it isn't either," he added, as a memory struck him. "I'm due to be out of a job as soon as my boss hears how I have failed over here. So this less than forty dollars represents not only my total cash assets, but my prospects as well."

He spoke lightly, but there was an undercurrent far

beneath the surface of his flippancy that reached the girl's heart. Keenly she eyed him for a moment. Then she said:

"Tell me."

Briefly, concisely, yet fully, he told her who he was and of his mission to Europe.

He said nothing of Phyllis Belden—not through desire for concealment, but because the secret was not his. Phyllis had bound both him and herself to secrecy as to their engagement. The fact that she had broken her part of the compact in telling Brant Ulrich of the affair did not seem to Garth a justification to himself for breaking his own pledge of silence.

But he told all the rest of the sorry tale, including his several interviews with Macbeath and his last night's escape from bondage. He ended with an account of the theft of his luggage and valuables from the Ferrol railroad station.

The positions of the two changed, without the conscious knowledge of either, during his short recital. At its conclusion they were standing close together in the hollow, and somehow their hands had become interclasped. Thus they stood for a few seconds after Garth had finished speaking.

Kathleen started back, as if waking from sleep. Gently she withdrew her hands from the man's grasp into which they had crept as he talked, but her eyes were soft and shining.

"It sounds like a lie," Roy began, gloomily, "and I can't expect you to believe it, but—"

"I do believe it!" she cried, in eager acceptance. "I do

believe it, Roy. You know I do. Oh, you poor, *poor* boy! You poor gallant boy! I'm—"

"Thanks," he said, shortly, his voice not all steady. "That pays for the whole thing. It makes it all worth while. Of course I haven't any proof to offer you, but—"

"Proof!" she repeated in high scorn. "As if I need 'proof!' You men are always harping on proof and on logic and all that! But a woman's intuition clears the whole journey at one stride, while proof and logic are still stumbling along, an inch at a time. Don't insult yourself, or me, by talking about 'proof,' Roy."

"I think," he said, chokingly—"I think I am happier than ever I dreamed I could be. I didn't think anyone could believe in me like that. It makes me ashamed that I'm not better worth it. . . . I told you your eyes always make me feel as if I were in church. I wish—"

He broke off, catching himself by sharp recollection of Phyllis Belden and of the wrong he was doing her by letting his heart and soul go out so to this clear-eyed Scottish girl. To change the dangerous theme he said in sudden remorse:

"But here I've been telling you about myself and whining for your trust and your sympathy, and all the time it is *you* who need comforting! You were crying when I came here. God knows I don't want to intrude on your trouble unless I can be of help. But I think you know I'd give anything in the world to help."

She reddened. Then her eyes met his, squarely as a boy's, and she made answer in all simplicity:

"I was crying because I believed I had been horribly mistaken in you. And I was crying because I knew you were in danger—for Mr. Ulrich has offered a personal reward of two hundred pounds to the constables to arrest you. And I was crying because I thought I was never going to see you again. I—"

With a wordless cry he broke in on her amazing confession, so frankly and quietly spoken. He took an impulsive step toward her, his arms half outstretched. Then his hands fell heavily to his side. His face went grim and he turned away.

She looked at him in troubled appeal. As he did not speak nor stir, she went on in a half-ashamed defiance:

"I can tell you something more: Do you know where we are? This is the Blasted Heath. You've read about it in 'Macbeth.' The witches used to haunt this hollow we're standing in. It was here they met King Macbeth, after the battle at Forres when he beat the Norwegian pirates. That's in the Macbeth play, too. It was here his son, Hamish MacBheathaig, met the witches on his way home to Cawdor, and here he heard the prophecy about the 'Luck of the Laird' depending on his collies."

"But—"

"Hielanders think it still is haunted," she continued. "The peasants say the witches are here, invisible, and that if anyone in sorrow comes here and asks them a favor, they may grant it if they are in good humor. Of course, that is foolish superstition. But when people are in trouble they aren't ashamed to turn to superstition or to any other strange hope, are they? I came here early this morning, and I made a wish. I wished I could see you again and that I could believe in you again. Honestly I did, Roy."

She spoke as simply and with as much freedom from coquetry as a child. Her words went through the man like the breath of God. He clenched his fists till the nails bit into his palms as he fought for self-control and as he sought in vain to conjure up the once-glamorous memory of the girl to whom he was betrothed. Then a wave of strange happiness swept over him.

"I am going to win!" he told her, half savagely. "I'm going to *win*. I don't know how, but I'm going to. I know it. The way to win this fight is not to hide out here like a licked puppy. I'm going to find Stirling, first of all. When I've found him, it'll be up to me to get him safely to America in spite of Brant Ulrich and in spite of Macbeath. I can figure out my line of action when I've found the dog. Have you any idea where he's hidden? Don't tell me if you'd rather not or if you think it is disloyal."

"I would be more loyal to my uncle by keeping him from a dishonest deed than to help him in it by not telling you," she made reply. "All I know is that Stirling wasn't at the castle the night you left. Uncle told me he had sent him with Comyn to help out for a week in driving the sheep to the pastures on Cateran Mountain for the spring grazing. He said Comyn's collie, Glamis, had gone lame. So—"

"Where is Cateran Mountain?"

"About seven or eight miles the other side of Thross. But—"

"That's where I'm off to, then," he said, making ready to climb out of the hollow. "I can go close to Thross. It would be safe enough, I suppose, to go straight through it. It's the last place they'd expect me to be. By this time the constables are probably hunting for me ten miles from there. It may be a false clue I'm on, but it's the only one. If Stirling isn't on Cateran Mountain, I can start my search over again. Good-by. You're not to worry about me. And—and I can't say what I want to, about the way your faith has made a new man of me. I—"

Abruptly he ran up the side of the hollow and set off toward the distant village. He heard her cry of protest, but he dared not answer it, nor so much as turn back to look at her.

Down the long slope of barren heath he ran, and along the peat-piled bottomland at the bog's edge, thence entering a twisted fold of the moor that brought him out, at last, on open and level ground a few miles from Thross.

Here the path widened into a rough moor road of sorts. Ahead, some distance beyond the next rise, was the village, cut off from view by the crest of the low swell of ground.

A mile to the left, a town of tents and booths had sprung into life on the flat moor, since last Garth had taken this indirect route to Thross.

For a moment Roy stared in surprise at the array of

tent peaks and flags and at the slowly expanding bulk of a mammoth captive balloon amid the cluster of impromptu shelters.

Then as the far-off strains of three merry-go-rounds came to him, mixed with the faint-heard cries of cheapjacks and barkers, and as he noted the throngs of holiday folk who were converging toward the tents from every direction, he knew this must be the yearly Spring Holiday Fair to which Kathleen had hoped he might take her.

He favored the scene of festivity with no more than a passing glance, after that, but breasted the gentle rise leading toward Thross.

Over the crest, from the direction of the village, an ancient motor car came jolting down the grade. It descended the slope directly toward him. When it was but fifty yards away someone in it gave a shout. The voice was Brant Ulrich's. Brant was in the tonneau, with two thickset men in uniform. A third uniformed man was sitting beside the driver.

Ulrich leaped up, pointing triumphantly toward Garth and bawling to the constables something whose nature Roy could only guess. The voice was as of a man who sets dogs after an alley cat.

The constables leaned forward. The driver put on all speed. Down upon the cornered fugitive roared and clanked the battered car with its load of man hunters.

CHAPTER TWELVE

——————

Down upon the luckless Garth rushed and wheezed the ancient police car. Ulrich and the three constables were on their feet ready to spring out and seize him as soon as the rattle-trap machine should come to a halt where he stood in the middle of the rutted moorland road. The car was barely twenty feet from him when Roy went into action.

It is only in story books that one unarmed man, be he ever so athletic, can hold his own against four stalwart opponents. Also, it was no part of Garth's program to be laid by the heels before he should have a chance to find Stirling or before the cabled money should arrive.

Flight was the sole solution. Wheeling, he left the road and sprinted across the uneven and rocky heath in the direction of the Spring Holiday Fair and its milling crowds.

In open country it would be only a matter of time before the car should overhaul him. The confusing crowds of the mile-distant fair promised a bare possibility of blocking the chase, and of permitting him to escape unseen from an opposite end of the fairgrounds.

Wherefore, with all his trained speed Garth made for

the straggly cluster of tents in whose center the captive balloon was tugging at its moorings.

The police car's chauffeur turned off the road and set forth across the field in hot pursuit of the racing American. Ulrich yelled furious encouragement to his companions, standing swayingly upright and pointing with his arms at the refugee.

But a rough Highland moor makes an ill racing course for any car. The ancient machine swung and bumped and all but stalled, over the innumerable obstacles. Once or twice it almost caught up with Roy. Oftener it lagged well behind.

Losing and gaining, Garth sped over the uneven ground. He was a practiced cross-country runner, and he was calling on every atom of speed and skill he possessed.

Yet he dived into the outer fringe of the crowd with scarce ten yards to spare. It was at a point where hundreds of moor-dwellers stood gaping up at the monster balloon. They had no eyes or ears for anyone or anything less than this gigantic miracle.

The shabby moth-eaten bag was full of gas at last. It was ready for its exhibition flight. In the balloon's basket stood its pilot, clad in tights and spangles, giving orders to men who held the mooring ropes and who leaned back, bracing themselves with heels dug into the turf and awaiting the word to cast off.

As Garth plowed his way through the crowd, the pilot's lips parted for this final order. Brant Ulrich, well ahead of the constables, caught up with Roy and seized him by the collar.

Eel-like and acting wholly on the escape instinct, Garth shed the coat and made one bound for the nearest balloon rope. An instant later, he scrambled to the edge of the basket just as the pilot bade the men cast off.

The balloonist had his back to Garth and Ulrich. With one foot poised theatrically on the basket's edge, he gave his order. As it was obeyed, the basket gave a sharp unexpected lurch, due to the weight of Garth's vaulting body.

This joggle was too much for the balloonist's pose and for his balance. Overside he tumbled, landing in a spread-eagle heap among the spectators.

Up shot the released balloon, the fat gray bag spinning slightly as it rose. Roy made shift to work his way over the perilously swinging edge and to drop panting into the bottom of the basket.

The motion was as of a ship in a heavy sea. The bag did not seem to him to be rising, but merely to pitch the light basket from side to side in nauseous iteration. Yet, as Roy peered overside, he saw the earth was receding from his view at dizzy speed.

There below him was the group of rustics, merging into a pinkish expanse of upturned blank faces. He could make out the bespangled pilot disengaging himself from a huddle of arms and legs and screeching inaudible curses or advice up at him. He could see Ulrich and the constables and the deserted motor car.

Then they were indistinguishable details in a blur of pink faces and dark clothes. The fair was spread below him like a badly drawn map, with its booths and tents and raree shows and merry-go-rounds and its antlike visitors.

Next, this too became a receding blur and the vast sweep of moorland was all around him. To the south, and seemingly close to the blob of fair ground, Macbeath Castle appeared on the rock it crowned, with a toy village straggling about its base.

Beyond and beyond and beyond rolled the sweep of moor and hillock and plain, girt in by the glittering vastnesses of snow-capped mountains.

The gas bag had flown straight upward in that first spin which had rocked the basket so sickeningly. Below, the air had been pleasantly warm under the morning sun. Now a chill struck through the coatless passenger's clothes to his perspiring body. The mile run had heated him uncomfortably. He was becoming more than uncomfortably cold.

An upper current of air, icy and strong, slapped the plump gray side of the bag, causing it to careen drunkenly and then blunder off to northward. The slap also jarred Garth wellnigh overside. He hung on for dear life, fighting with nausea and panic.

Lashed to an inner side of the basket was a thick frieze coat, evidently worn by the balloon's pilot in just such chilly air strata as this. With one hand Roy undid the straps and managed to wriggle into the rough garment.

Then he used the same lashings to fasten himself to one of the basket's inner iron rings.

Warmer and in no immediate peril of being knocked overboard, he had leisure to look about him again and to accustom himself to viewing the earth without a shudder, from this dizzy height.

Like some stupid and overfed bumblebee, the balloon was bungling along, the sport of the stiffening air currents, ever crawling higher, ever forced northward.

Far below, Roy could see the prim gray outlines of Cawdor Castle and its lovely grounds. Highroads and byroads lay athwart the country's checkered surface like aimless gray cobweb threads.

He made out a sweep of hill with young tree-plantations pressing up its sides, then a road and a monument and a scatter of hewn stones beyond it.

He knew thus that he was soaring above the battlefield of Culloden where he and Kathleen had picnicked so happily only a few days before.

Soon appeared the picturesque alignment of houses and cottages and streetlets that marked the waterside-resort town of Nairn. Below, to the left, spread Inverness, capital of the Highlands. Beyond it shone and sparkled the fire-blue waters of Moray Firth.

And now Inverness and Nairn were behind him, and the balloon was rollicking clumsily out far above the Firth.

"If we've got to drop at all," remarked Garth, as if to some human companion, "this would be the least worse place, I suppose. I'd land softer on the water than on a mountain top."

He spoke aloud to buoy up his own spirit. The sound of his voice, reedy and indistinct at this altitude amid the rushing of the wind, gave him reassurance and made him feel less as though he were in some impossible nightmare. Wherefore he spoke again.

"But we must be a good mile above ground," he went on, "and at that height probably it wouldn't matter a whole lot whether it was water or land we connected with, in a drop. . . . The North Sea is out yonder, in the direction we're going. If we have luck we may get clear across to Norway before we collapse. If we don't —well, there's plenty of room for us in the sea. Better men than I have gone to sleep there."

This form his soliloquy had taken was not cheering, so he shifted his thoughts to his immediate surroundings. Never before had he made a balloon ascension. Vaguely he remembered reading or hearing somewhere that sand is thrown out to make the bag go higher and gas is let out of the bag to make it sink.

But he saw no sand bags among the basket's confusing litter of contents. Neither did he see any labeled gas valve to turn on, in order to descend. He began looking morbidly up at the incredibly huge bulge of gray net-covered cloth above him. There were patches here and there on its swollen surface. The material looked dangerously old and insecure, as if it might burst at any time under the internal pressure of its gas.

Sometimes the basket spun. Sometimes it rocked. Only at brief intervals did it remain stabilized. During these intervals Garth forgot to gasp with nausea and he looked down on the fast-moving world below him.

Perhaps some upper air current was influenced by the water beneath. At any rate, the balloon had been following the course of Moray Firth, keeping directly above the inlet. Now the gray-blue expanse of the North Sea loomed on all sides, with no visible land ahead.

Trawlers, no larger than ducks, bobbed far below on the sea's surface. A yacht, with billowy snow-white canvas all set, careened across the ripples farther out toward the hazy horizon line. The water's surface was wrinkled, like finger tips that have been in hot suds.

"I wish I remembered enough geography to know how wide the North Sea is, between Scotland and Norway," mused Garth. "And I wish I had bothered to ask, sometime, how long one of these old-style gas bags stays in the air before it does its flop. Still," he added, philosophically, "I'm due to find out one or both those things before the day is over."

Mechanically he felt for his pipe. Then he remembered it and his tobacco pouch were both in a pocket of the coat he had shucked when Ulrich nabbed him. His matches were in their metal case in his trousers pocket, but there was nothing for them to light. Then, with recurring philosophy, he reflected he was far too seasick to have enjoyed a smoke even if he had had the materials for one.

Dispassionately he fell to wondering what would happen at Thross, now that he was removed definitely from the contest. Would Ulrich's cash and Ulrich's craft avail to get Stirling from Macbeath and to bring the dog home in triumph to America, there to clean up at every big show and to keep the Beldencroft collies in the second-rater division?

And how about Phyllis? How deeply and how long would she mourn her vanished wooer, the man who had perished on the mission whose prize was to have been her hand?

But, to his annoyance, as ever lately, Garth's brain would not focus on the girl to whom he was betrothed. Instead it veered instantly and persistently to Kathleen Macbeath.

"Well," he assured himself, "there can't be anything disloyal to Phyll, now, in my letting myself think of *her*. I'm past the zone of loyalties and disloyalties."

His mind began to reconstruct, in every detail, his scene with Kathleen in the witches' hollow on the Blasted Heath that morning. The keenness and beauty of the memory made him forget his present hopeless condition and the doom that lay before him somewhere beyond that hazy North Sea horizon.

How long he floated between sky and sea he did not know. An apathy began to creep over him. At that great height, the cold bit through the thick frieze coat he had found.

There was something that looked like a rug lashed to

another side of the basket. He unfastened it. Not only was it a frayed lap-rug still fairly thick in spite of its age, but it was wrapped around a paper parcel that gave forth a gurgling sound as it rolled from Roy's lap to the bottom of the basket.

Garth retrieved it and opened it. It contained a quart bottle of cold black coffee and eight large greasy sandwiches. The balloonist's projected lunch, no doubt. The sight of it reminded Garth that he himself had not eaten for nearly twenty-four hours.

Forgotten were his dumb nausea and his dizziness. With raw animal appetite he began to devour the thick sandwiches and to gulp the strong black coffee. For a space he gave no thought to his desperate plight, but used his every faculty in the enjoyment of this sorely needed food and drink.

The meal acted like a tonic on his nerves and spirits. Gone was his seasickness. He felt all at once strong and hopeful again, ready to meet whatever fate might be in store; to meet it fighting—fighting not grimly but in gay defiance.

He looked overside. The white-sailed yacht was in the same direction from him as before, but much farther away. Puzzled, he looked out at the other side. The shores of Scotland once more were clearly visible. Either the wind had shifted or else the bag had risen or sunk to a different current of air; a current that was carrying it back along its former route.

Somehow the change seemed to Roy a good omen.

With increasing interest he watched the Firth reappear beneath him. He could make out the taller spires of Inverness.

Then the balloon was over the land again, not following its former course, but sailing bumpily above Loch Ness. The lake lay below Roy's gaze like a long blue lozenge amid the brown and soft green of its hills and dales, with the surrounding lesser lakes spattering the spring landscape's maplike expanse.

Southward, toward Pitlochry and the pass of Killicrankie, the balloon was butting its erratic way; above glorious countryside smiling to new life after the rigor of the northland winter.

The air was warmer, here in the upper reaches of the bag's course, or else the balloon had blundered into a warm stratum and was being held there.

A full meal and the lulling motion of the basket made Garth increasingly drowsy. He was keenly in need of sleep. With a new-found philosophy he told himself that he would neither be adding to nor subtracting from his dire peril by resisting this craving for slumber.

Curling up as comfortably as he could in the bottom of the basket, he went to sleep.

Now and then an especially rough jounce of the balloon, as it was slapped by a cross-current of air, roused him halfway and momentarily to his senses; as the jar of a switching engine may half arouse slumbrous Pullman passengers at night. But for the most part he slept soundly and heavily; nature completing the cure begun by his hearty luncheon.

He awoke, hours later, stiff and cold, but infinitely refreshed. Peering out, he saw that the dusk was settling. He did not know where he might be, except that water glimmered again beneath the basket. Whether he was above a loch or over the North Sea he had no way of guessing.

But one fact was sharply apparent—the balloon was many hundred feet nearer the earth than when he had gone to sleep. Hitherto, the neat hill fields and even the mountain tops had looked like the patterns of a bas-relief map. Now, despite the dimness about him, he could make out detail after detail that had been invisible at his former immense height.

He saw a fishing boat in the water, and he could see the faces of the two men in her as they stared blankly up at the gray flabby bag bobbing along over their heads.

Then he saw a huge fish break water in a curving leap. But presently the fast-gathering dusk hemmed him in and hid all distant objects.

Roy groped about the basket until he found two sandwiches he had not eaten at noon. He devoured them both and finished the last swig of the strong unsweetened coffee. By the time he looked about him again black night had shut out all view.

Clouds covered the whole sky. The balloon was lurching and heaving drunkenly through impenetrable blackness.

Whether he rode so for an hour or for two hours Roy did not know. As during his first moments in the air, he had no sensation of moving at all, except for the spin and swing of the basket. Nor had these the vehemence of the former oscillations. There was a sagging listlessness about them.

There was no way of gauging the balloon's speed, in the pitch dark, by objects on the earth or water below. It might be whizzing along at sixty miles an hour or it might be almost motionless.

The man lost all sense of time or of motion. He knew only that he was hanging between earth and sky or between water and sky, and that he was as helpless as any ant caught up in a typhoon.

He wondered how long the basket and the collapsing bag could keep afloat if they should come down in sea or loch, and how hard they would smite the ground if they should descend on mountain top or in a forest.

Then he was knocked forward on his face. The spinning basket had struck heavily against some hard surface and its course had been checked. With utter absence of motion it lodged there, while the half-empty bag waved and sagged and flapped above it in the dense darkness.

Roy put forth exploratory hands. His groping fingers told him the basket had stranded amid flat-sided rocks and that the wind's pushing of the gas bag was holding the car tight against a projection above the rocks.

Here, if ever, was Garth's chance to escape from the soaring coffin wherein he had been immured since long before noon. Nimbly he unfastened his lashings. Nimbly he swarmed overside and dropped safely on a flat slab of rock.

At once the almost deflated bag, relieved of his weight, lurched upward, its basket following in wabbly deliberation. Bag and basket vanished into the night, leaving their passenger stranded on the rock to whose solid surface he had dropped.

His wild voyage was over. Whether he had landed on the inaccessible topmost peak of some snow-capped mountain or on a valley's pile of cairn stones, at least he was free from the terror of the sky. His feet were planted on honest earth-imbedded rock, not on the plunging floor of a balloon basket. He was safe.

What matter was it whether he had debarked on hilltop or vale; in Scotland or in Norway? He was alive. Tumultuous happiness surged through him at the sudden reaction from peril. To his knees he sank, his head bowed in a wordless prayer of gratitude for his deliverance.

Then, rising, he looked around. Everywhere the pitchy darkness shut him in. The night wind whispered caressingly about him. For all he knew he might well be at the brink of some precipice. Wherefore he began to shuffle forward with consummate care, his arms in front of him.

At his second cautious step his toe came against something unyielding, but which had not the uncompromising hardness of rock. He bent and felt for it. His fingers ran along a smooth wooden surface, square as a box top. At one side he felt a pair of rusted hinges.

Garth frowned in bewilderment. On rocky mountain tops or on rock slabs in plains, one did not expect to find a hinged box top fastened into place. It savored of Ali Baba's visit to the cave of the Forty Thieves.

Impelled by a childish curiosity, Roy ran his fingers to the side of the top farthest from the hinges, and sought to lift it. At his second tug the lid gave way and arose under the tugging of his strong fingers.

It was then that he thought for the first time of his matches. But he did not light one of them until he had explored with an arm under the opened lid. Apparently the square of wood masked or covered a well of some kind; for there was a vacant space as far down as Garth's arm could reach.

Then his fingers brushed a clean-cut corner of stone down there, and another above it. He made out the contour of stone steps. A stairway led from the surface downward, perhaps into the bowels of the earth.

His curiosity piqued, Roy let himself down into the narrow chasm, his feet finding their balance on the stone stairway. When he had descended far enough to be out of the wind, he lighted a match.

The yellow flare showed him he was near the bottom of a short flight of steps which ended in a stone-floored space perhaps eight feet square. In one side of this chamber and directly opposite the steps was a small iron-bound oaken door, old and massive.

There was a hammered-iron latch in the door. Roy stepped forward and pressed it down, at the same time putting his shoulder to the upper panel.

Creakingly the thick door opened inward under his push.

From just beyond the portal came a most unearthly sound. It was something between a deep throated growl and a wild-beast snarl.

Roy leaped back from the door, his heels striking the steps behind him with a force that threw him off his balance. He sat down very hard indeed, and quite involuntarily, on one of the stairs.

Before he could struggle to his feet, or could reach the sinister door in front of him to bar out the mysterious snarling creature on its far side, he heard the hinges creak again as the Thing pushed its fierce way through toward him.

CHAPTER THIRTEEN

—————

UP GARTH leaped, to fight back the invisible enemy that was charging out at him. Then, in a trice, the murderous growl merged into a whine of eager friendliness. The creature was capering about Roy in the dark, sniffing his hands and leaping joyously upon him.

Dizzy with relief and ashamed of his own momentary superstitious fears, Garth grasped the animal as it planted its forepaws on his chest. His fingers touched the chiseled silken head of a collie.

He had known what manner of beast it was, ever since that eager whimper of greeting had sounded. But the feel of its head and ruff awoke in him a crazy hope. Tremblingly he struck another match. Then he babbled, aloud:

"Stirling! Lord! but it's *Stirling!*"

At the calling of his name the great dog rubbed his cold muzzle playfully against Roy's hand, laying his head on the man's knee. He was overjoyed to see this new human friend of his, though already he was a bit ashamed —as befits a dignified collie—of his own whining and capering outburst of welcome.

Garth stood staring down at the dog, incredulous. Then the last flicker of his match lighted the room beyond—the room through whose narrow doorway the collie had bounded to meet him.

It was somewhat larger than the one into which Roy had descended through the wooden lid's aperture. In one corner was a tousled bed of straw. Beside it were a pail of water and a half-eaten dog dinner of meat and table scraps. A shut door at each side of this larger room led to unknown regions.

In a flash Roy Garth guessed precisely where he must be and how he had come thither.

It was no mountain crag or valley cairn he had landed on, from the balloon. After the bag's aimless aerial wanderings, wafted and slapped hither and yon by a dozen baffling and conflicting currents of the upper air, it had drifted back—as so often happens—to within a few miles of the spot whence its flight had begun.

Flying low, it had grazed the top of a low castle on a low hill. Its basket had become caught against one of the turret's crenelations, until the removal of Roy's weight had enabled the gas bag to lift it onward again.

Garth had been set down upon the turret, whence, by opening the scuttle door, he had descended into the interior. Well did he know that there was but one castle thereabouts in whose disused turret rooms Stirling was likely to be concealed.

Yes, Garth's crazy wanderings in the upper ether had brought him back and set him down in the one spot on earth that he had most desperate reason to avoid.

He was in the turret of Macbeath Castle!

Fate had played one more of her most choicely ironical jokes on the American, in carrying him all over the Highlands and far out above the sea, and then depositing him gently in the very abode of those who sought his undoing.

Roy stood dumfounded at the realization, his hand still stroking absentmindedly the head of the collie. Then the daze passed, leaving him joyously alert and excited.

"Stirling, old friend," he whispered, the humor of the situation making him hard put to it to choke back a laugh, "this morning I started out to hunt for you. Everything hung on my finding you and then getting safe away with you. Well, by some inordinate luck I've found you. Now to get you out of here and on the way to the nearest railroad station before they can lay us by the heels. It's about fifty to one against, old fellow."

The collie's plumed tail wagged appreciatively at Roy's repetition of his name.

"But up to now it's been a *billion* to one against," continued Roy. "At this rate, pretty soon I'll be a favorite in the betting. Come along, and don't make any racket. If we're to get safe away from this comic-opera villain's den, we've got to do it on tiptoe. If we're caught, all sorts of things are due to happen. And—they won't all of them happen to *us*, either."

He lighted another match. Then, his hand on the dog's ruff, he entered the larger room and looked at each of its side-wall doors in turn.

Both doors doubtless led downstairs to the living quarters of the castle. Thus, out of either, there must be egress to the moor beyond, if one were not detected en route.

Macbeath, evidently, had hidden Stirling in the turret until chance of his recapture by Garth should be past. Not even Kathleen knew where he was concealed. Also, the dog had been well fed and watered in his temporary prison. The food dishes attested to that.

Someone must come here daily to bring him his meals. By which egress would Roy and Stirling be least likely to run into whatever person had access to the turret rooms? Garth tried the left-hand door. It was locked or barred on the far side. But the right-hand door yielded to his pressing of its latch. The problem of which door to choose had settled itself.

Still holding Stirling's ruff, Garth made his way down a second and somewhat longer flight of stone steps. At the bottom he found himself in a passageway that ran in either direction. To the left, it seemed to lead toward the hall. Here, at this hour, presumably, members of the household or else the servants might be encountered.

Garth chose the right-hand passage. Stealthily he tiptoed along it, the dog at his side. A door barred his way. It was unlocked. He passed over its threshold as his last match flickered out.

Experimentally, Roy stepped out into the wide room that the match's final flare had shown indistinctly to him. Stirling held back. Garth chirped to him. The dog followed, though with very apparent reluctance.

The flooring sloped unaccountably downward. It

seemed to sag and to waver under the tread of the man and the dog.

"I've still got my 'air legs,' " thought Roy. "Even this stone floor heaves when I walk on it. I—"

With a low rending the floor opened beneath his feet. Amid a choking cloud of dust, he and Stirling pitched downward through space.

Brant Ulrich and Macbeath had finished a late and leisurely dinner. They were sitting in front of the study fireplace, liqueurs and cigars on the tabouret between them. Tonight Kathleen was not at her piano. Directly after dinner she had gone to her room.

"By this time, then," Ulrich was saying, contemplatively, "he and the balloon will both be somewhere at the bottom of the North Sea? I suppose you can trust the man who sent you the telegram about seeing the balloon headed straight for Norway?"

"As Macrue is the one person within fifty miles who owes me money, instead of my owing it to him," answered the Laird, "I think we may bank on his not daring to lie to me. Besides, he is a man who never tells unnecessary lies. I suppose he thinks it might spoil his style for the necessary ones. . . . Not that I condemn anyone for an occasional lie, if it be artistic and useful. No man who is not ashamed to lock the door of his strong box with a key need be ashamed to lock the door of his mind with a lie."

" 'A man's a man, for a' that,' " returned Ulrich, bored

by his host's long disquisition. "I think that's the way your Scotch Tommy Burns puts it. He—"

A grunt of horrified contempt from the Laird interrupted him. Macbeath was glaring at his guest with all a Highlander's loathing for an outlander who bungles the name or the verses of the idolized Scottish poet. In his indignation the chief lapsed into almost broad dialect.

"'Tommy' Burns!" he rumbled. "'*Tommy*' Burns, heh? Syne ye'll be blithering aboot 'Isadore' Shakespeare and 'Charley' the Baptist. '*Tommy*'—"

Somewhat to his relief, the butler came in through the passageway from the pantry.

"Excuse me, sir," said the servant, "but the taxicab is here with the Ferrol station master. There was a robbery of the parcel room at the railway station there, last night. Mr. Garth's luggage was stored there, the station master says; and it was stolen. This afternoon the thieves were caught in a room they had hired, and all the stolen things were found. The station master thought Mr. Garth was still staying here. So, after work hours he drove over here himself with his things. What'll I tell him, sir?"

"Tell him to dump them all in the loch!" snapped Macbeath. "And tell him if he's expecting a tip from me for bringing—"

"Hold on!" cut in Ulrich, unceremoniously silencing his host. "That's nonsense. Listen, my man," he went on to the butler. "Did you see the luggage, yourself?"

"Yes, sir," said the butler. "He was setting it on the steps when I went out to see him. He—"

"Was there a small handbag with it?"

"Yes, sir. And all the luggage he had when he was staying here."

The eyes of Macbeath and Ulrich met.

"Give the station master three pounds for his trouble," ordered Brant, "and thank him. Here's the money. Then bring all the luggage in here at once. Quick!"

The butler departed sullenly. He did not relish taking orders from an outlander, in his laird's presence. Macbeath favored his guest with a glower that held no favor at all. During the past few hours the American giant with his amused patronage and his domineering manner had been getting on the old chief's nerves and temper.

But the glower died, scarce born. He gave mental homage to Ulrich's cleverness in ordering all Garth's luggage brought to them. Unquestionably, Roy's more important valuables would be among it; presumably, as Ulrich had guessed, in the small handbag.

It would be a ridiculously simple thing to open the luggage and to hunt until Stirling's "papers" were found, then to destroy them and with them the haunting danger of legal punishment. Without these proofs, Roy, if he still lived, would be powerless to claim the dog or to demand back his ten thousand dollars.

Or—still shrewder plan!—it would be a matter of less than twenty minutes to make out a set of duplicate papers, substituting the name of Glamis for Stirling.

The Laird came closer to smiling than for days.

Back plodded the butler. He was convoying the apelike porter, who deposited on the study table the armful of luggage.

"The station master brought over the mail bag, too, sir," reported the butler, handing his master several loose letters and a small packet of envelopes tied together. "The ones in the bundle are from America, for Mr. Garth. They were addressed to him at the Goat & Compasses Inn, sir; but the station master thought he was staying here, so he left them."

The butler busied himself with mending the hearth fire. Macbeath fidgeted. He did not want to rouse suspicion by ordering the man from the room, and he dared not begin the task of rifling Garth's luggage while this unnecessary witness was present. In another minute he would be gone, so the chief possessed himself in such patience as he could.

" 'The Goat & Compasses!' " laughed Brant Ulrich, as eager as Macbeath to get at the bags, but enjoying the old man's annoyance. " 'Goat & Compasses!' What insane-asylum graduate named your Scotch inns, anyhow, Chief? And yesterday I passed by 'The Pig & Whistle.' Idiotic, *I* call it."

"You call it so," rapped out Macbeath, "because you know nothing at all about it. The Thross Inn, during the Covenanter days, was piously named 'God Encompass Us!' It was corrupted into 'Goat & Compasses.' As for the 'Pig & Whistle,' that started life, three hundred years ago, as 'The Pagan Wassail.' So— Ah! He's gone at last, the slow-poke donkey! Now, are we to slit these bags or break the locks? I must yield to your greater experience in such matters. I shall be proud to take a lesson of an expert. Do we want a knife, or have you your skeleton keys with you?"

"I'm sorry, Chief," returned Brant in entire good humor, "but I didn't bring any skeleton keys across the ocean with me. I knew they wouldn't be needed among a people whose every lock responds to a gold key. I'll try my knife to the leather of this," he went on, picking up the small handbag. "I've a grudge against this satchel. It nearly broke my skull, once. Always I meant to pay that debt, with compound interest. But today the North Sea has paid it for me. If I'm not mistaken, we'll find everything we want in here, without going through the rest of the luggage. I left my penknife in my lounge clothes. Suppose you just hand me that property *sgian dhu*, tucked in your stocking? If it has any sort of edge to it—"

"To slit a filthy handbag with?" rebuked Macbeath, savage again on the instant. "A chief's *sgian dhu* has no rightful scabbard but its own and the flesh of an enemy. Maybe you'll suggest we use my two historic claymores, on the wall, yon, to carve the joint with, at dinner tomorrow?"

"If the meat is as tough as the venison we had for dinner tonight," responded Ulrich, smilingly, as he glanced up at the crossed straight swords with their basket hilts, on the wall behind him, "I'd suggest dynamite. I think you said your ancestor carried those swords in the Prince

Charlie campaign, didn't you, Chief? Must have been a bloodthirsty old rascal, to need two swords for two successive battles! If the campaign had lasted much longer, he'd have had to stay out of the fighting, because all his swords would have been in the wash."

The Laird's face hardened, but he showed no other sign of his hot resentment at the foreigner's flippant slur on sacred Macbeath family traditions. From his sporran he took a keen-edged penknife and handed it unopened to Brant.

"Suppose we drop the airy persiflage and do the dirty work we are here to do," he said.

Ulrich opened the knife. Putting the handbag between his knees, he drew the blade across the handbag's tough surface. Under his powerful hand the pigskin was cut clean through, laying open the entire side of the receptacle. Holding the gap apart, Brant shook the bag's contents out onto the table.

The green-bound passport tumbled forth, and after it a fat roll of express checks, several thick envelopes, and last of all a well-used and well-filled black wallet. Tossing aside the empty satchel, Brant picked up the wallet, opening it and rummaging its contents.

The Laird watched him with an eagerness that was more than tinged with contempt at the dishonorable deed he himself was countenancing. Ulrich fished forth from the wallet a neatly-banded little sheaf of papers and glanced through them.

"Here we are!" he exclaimed. "The whole works, all

fastened together—bill of sale, transfer, receipt, certified pedigree and all."

"Give them to me," said Macbeath, his disgust lost in the joyful relief of having the incriminating documents back in his own possession.

He reached forth a clawlike hand to receive them. But Ulrich pocketed them.

"I think I'll just keep these for the present," smilingly explained Brant, in response to the Laird's command and gesture. "They may come in handy in case you decide to double cross me as you double crossed that poor fool who is feeding the North Sea fishes. These will be a very sweet safeguard for—"

The sagging canvas ceiling above him ripped clean across. Down into the study crashed two bodies in a cloud of dust—a man's and a dog's.

Garth and the collie had been close side by side when the rotting canvas gave way under them. Thus, close together, they landed from their fall. By rare good luck their drop was broken by an obstacle slightly softer than the stone flooring. They struck it at the same time.

The obstacle chanced to be Brant Ulrich's broad back as he leaned over to pick up the slit handbag.

Under the double weight, Brant collapsed to the stones, the breath knocked out of him, his nose broken by the impact with the stone floor.

The dazzle of light, after so long a time in darkness, half-blinded Roy. Winking hard, he staggered to his feet seeking to adjust his widened eye pupils to the new illumination.

A wrought fire screen and a stand of armor had been knocked over by the jar of the triple crash. They clattered to the flagging with much din and reverberation.

So did the two Prince Charlie claymores. The loose nail from which the swords hung had yielded to the shaking of the whole room as the men and the dog fell together. The historic weapons clanged against the stones and rattled to a resting place beside the welter of struggling and scrambling bodies.

Brant Ulrich, on hands and knees, writhed free from the incumbrances that had felled him. The shock of the double collision, as well as the pain of his broken nose—an aristocratically modeled Grecian feature of which he was inordinately proud—had obsessed him with homicidal fury.

As he sprang up, his right hand's groping fingers closed around the basket hilt of one of the fallen claymores. It lay where his palm had encountered it in his effort of rising from all fours. He gripped the sword and leaped to his feet, glaring about him murderously.

It was then that he saw and recognized the blinking Roy. Brant's anger swelled to mania at the sight. With a roar he hurled himself at Garth, sword aloft.

It was this spectacle which Roy's eyes focused on as his vision accustomed itself to the light. He dodged backward from the onrushing menace. Yet he would not have been quick enough to avoid the swashing sweep of the claymore had not an ally intervened gallantly to help him.

Stirling had been less shaken by the tumble than had

been either of the two men. He had landed slantingly on Ulrich's hip and had bounced thence to the floor, landing lightly and with his feet under him. He had gotten up, and looked about him in pleased interest at finding himself snugly at home once more in his master's familiar study after his days of dull imprisonment.

The situation appealed strongly to the keen sense of the dramatic which is ever foremost in a collie's brain. Stirling was prepared to enjoy to the full his reunion with Macbeath and to receive much petting from Kathleen.

Then, at once, his gay air changed to wrathful astonishment. He saw his new human chum, Garth, who had rescued him from that lonely turret room; and he saw a huge and most dislikable stranger rushing at Garth as if to strike him with a gleaming stick of some kind.

That was too much for the loyal collie. He sprang, with the speed of a striking snake, full at Ulrich's throat. He missed the jugular by an inch. But his mighty jaws rent Brant's collar and tie away and tore his soft evening shirt from neck to waist.

What was more to the purpose, Stirling's seventy pounds of muscular furry weight smote the chest of the charging man with the force of a catapult.

Ulrich was halted, dead, in the midst of his onset. With one hand he sought to brush aside the rushing collie, while he turned ragingly again on Roy Garth. But the second or two of respite had sufficed.

Roy had sprung back out of reach, and his heel had

hit against the blade of the other claymore. Instantly he had snatched up the long-bladed sword and had thrown himself on guard.

With a homicidal devil dashing at him and brandishing a claymore, there was no scope for argument or for self-defense with bare fists. His one hope was to meet steel with steel.

Even as trivialities are forever darting into minds that are oppressed with sudden danger, Roy's thoughts went back to the Midwestburg Athletic Club, where, this very month, he and Ulrich were to have competed with each other for the club's annual trophies in broadsword fencing.

Here, more than four thousand miles from Midwestburg, they were face to face, broadswords in hand, competing for no mere tinsel cup, but for life itself.

Then there was no further chance for thought, whether relevant or irrelevant. Brant was upon him, attacking with a vehemence whose rage did not rob it of consummate skill and swordsmanship.

The two blades clashed together like living creatures. From their ringing contact a shower of red sparks spat forth into the air.

For the first time in nearly two hundred years the ancient war weapons were in use again; once more set to the task of taking human life, here in the Highlands where of old they had been forged and where they had drunk Lowland blood.

With clash and clang and slither the blades embraced

and parted and smote together again, whining one against the other in the eternal hate-song of the ages.

Arcs of white light flashed from them in the lamp glare, and once and again they sent forth their showering red sparks.

Roy had met his assailant's mad onset with a rocklike defense. Not one step did he fall back. Not one inch of ground did he yield as the giant pressed him furiously and launched a storm of lightning-swift and Hercules-strong swordsweeps at him.

Blade to blade, foot to foot, Garth opposed him, giving blow for blow, overcoming the momentary advantage of Ulrich's charge; parrying, cutting, lunging, riposting, with all the cool vigor he would have employed in the club's fencing room.

Stirling had been removed from the conflict immediately after his wild leap at Ulrich's throat. Macbeath had caught his dog by the scruff of the neck and dragged him back from the slaughter, holding him tightly and preventing him by hand and by voice from plunging into it again.

The Laird stood thus, gripping his wildly struggling collie and watching the ferocious duel with a smile of bland amusement on his thin old lips.

He was Highlander enough to revel in a fierce fight well waged. To his astonishment, he noted that both of these foreigners were swordsmen of the highest type, even when handling such an unfamiliar weapon as the cut-and-thrust claymore. The duel was going to be entertainingly worth witnessing.

Into Macbeath's memory came an ancient Highland tale of one Meg Dunoon, of Dalwhinny, who looked out of her farmhouse window and beheld her husband in death-battle with a bear. She had remarked, as she watched their combat:

"I care na' a crackit ha' penny which o' the twa may win. They're baith puir feckless caterans."

The blades locked, tore free, slashed and stabbed. The men's first moveless stance was broken. Both fighters were in motion now, their agile feet shifting them forward or back as they attacked or defended.

Ulrich's far greater height and longer reach were of mighty advantage to him in this bout, even as they had served to win him more than one cup in fencing tourneys at home.

Opposed to this, in Garth, was a physical strength equal to Brant's own, and a compact swiftness of motion that almost atoned for the other's greater height and reach.

And now Roy was taking full advantage of this superior quickness. He was everywhere and nowhere, fighting with wildcat savagery, yet warily on guard against the taller man's advantage of reach.

In and out he battled, holding his own as he and Brant stamped and slipped on the smooth-worn stone flagging and as their blades slithered and flashed and clanged.

Twice, by scarce more than a hair's breadth, he had warded or ducked sweeping strokes for his head—strokes which, had they reached their mark, would have cleft his skull from scalp to chin.

Once, in countering, his sword tip had all but found its sheath in the muscular throat of his adversary. It had penetrated Brant's neck for a fraction of an inch, drawing first blood.

The sting of the slight wound and his opponent's stubbornly clever fighting drove Ulrich to the verge of mania. His visage was distorted. His broken nose had begun to swell hideously. Blood from it was smearing his lower face.

A lesser man could not have maintained that whirlwind pace and spendthrift expenditure of power as did Ulrich. But as the duel progressed he seemed to wax stronger and faster and deadlier. Avidly he tore away at his smaller and swifter antagonist who danced so annoyingly just outside the thin edge of death.

Both men were panting now. Their ever-moving feet had twisted and snarled the deerskin rugs and had upset chairs and stools. Once they had caromed off the heavy refectory table, jarring an avalanche of its books and ornaments to the floor.

Up and down the long room they raged; slashing and thrusting and guarding, alternately charging and retreating.

In the bloodshot eyes of both blazed a deathless murderous hate. Their ancient rivalry, in love and in athletics, their innate dislike for each other, the wrongs and frustrations of the past few days—these and the magic of the naked blades had combined to strip from them the last shred of civilization's veneer, and to turn them into primordial foes with no wish nor thought save for each other's annihilation.

In this twelfth-century castle two modern human products of twentieth-century progress were adjusting their life-grudge by the instinctive method of prehistoric man.

The walls rang to the reverberant clash of steel. The ripped canvas ceiling sent down clouds of dust upon the fighters as each newly-overturned piece of furniture shook the room.

Choking with dust, adrip with sweat, panting and snarling, the two battled on.

A second time Garth's ever-darting swordpoint nicked its target, this time more deeply, scoring an ugly gouge in Ulrich's right cheek as Brant's sudden backward shift deflected it from his throat.

Howling with the pain and humiliation of this new touch, Ulrich threw away what semblance of caution he had used. He flew at Garth with an unceasing succession of blows, delivered with the speed of lightning.

Back moved Roy under this storm of assault, guarding adroitly and ever seeking an instant's let-up in the fiery onslaught or an opening through which he might slide his own snakelike swordpoint deep into the giant body that menaced him so murderously. Wisely, against this longer-reached antagonist, Garth was relying on the point, rather than on the edge of his weapon, for the offensive.

In lunging, Ulrich's right toe caught in a tangled deerskin. He stamped, to regain his balance. His left heel caught in another fold of the rug. Down he crashed in a heap among the tumble of skins and chairs.

"Now!" barked Macbeath, waving his free arm to Garth and then pointing to the fallen man whose claymore had flown from his balance-clutching fingers. "Now then, laddie! Finish the swine. Cut his fat throat!"

The Laird chuckled as Roy jumped to where his rabid foe lay trying to kick his feet free from the encumbering deerskin. But the chuckle died in a mumble of astonished contempt. For Roy merely stooped and jerked Ulrich to his feet, handing him his dropped sword.

Perhaps in his rage blindness Brant did not realize it was his enemy who had raised him and who had restored to him his lost weapon. Perhaps the jar and the shame of his clumsy fall had swept from him the last vestiges of sense and of humanity.

For he grabbed the proffered claymore and thrust viciously with it at Garth's unguarded heart.

Roy shrank nimbly aside, easily avoiding the awkward blow. Then, immediately, Ulrich was at him again as ferociously as before and as madly eager to slay his smaller opponent.

But the shock of the fall or else the incredible fighting pace he had maintained was abating Brant's earlier speed. He had lost his bewilderingly tigerish agility. He was slowing, weakening. Quick to note this, Roy forced the offensive; pressing Ulrich back and giving him all he could do to guard a lightning succession of thrusts.

Slower grew Ulrich's guard. Roy feinted for the throat, then twisted to a "moulinet," slashing with all his force at Brant's head.

It was a clever ruse. Almost it succeeded. More by luck than by deftness, Ulrich blocked the head slash. The blades met in a spark-showering clang as Brant guarded the mighty blow.

The contact snapped Garth's ancient claymore blade clean in two, close to the hilt.

CHAPTER FOURTEEN

THE steel tinkled to the floor. Roy gripped the useless hilt and stared foolishly on the treacherous blade. With a shout Ulrich swung his own claymore aloft and brought it down with clumsy pile-driver force at the disarmed man's skull.

But no longer was his power backed by any semblance of speed. Easily Roy ducked the smashing stroke and sprang in, tackling the giant about the lower body in dexterous football fashion. The sword blow whizzed harmlessly beyond him and the claymore's point snapped on the stone flagging.

As he gained his hold about his enemy's upper legs, Roy braced himself and heaved backward with a muscle-cracking vigor that strained his whole frame. Brant's forward-hurtling body doubled the momentum of the stupendous heave.

Back, over Roy's head spread-eagled the giant, cata-pulting through the air as if from a huge sling shot. His head smote against the stone jut of the chimneypiece with a sickening crash.

Thence he flopped limp to the floor, like a shot vulture, and lay there, sprawled and inert. A violent convulsive shiver went through him. Then he lay still.

(It was six weeks later, in an Edinburgh hospital, that Brant Ulrich opened his eyes again upon the world to which he had been restored by a delicate operation on his fractured skull. It was a full half year before he could walk upright and strong and whole as of old.)

Gasping, dizzy, faint, Garth reeled against the table and stood there, the big room swimming about him.

Vaguely he saw that the doorways were crowded with scared men- and maidservants, drawn thither by the din of battle.

Vaguely, too, his eye fell on a pile of luggage that seemed familiar. Then his wandering gaze fixed itself on his treasured and stolen handbag, slit open and empty. The sight concentrated his fatigue-scattered wits.

Macbeath had been leaning over the prostrate Ulrich, fumbling at the senseless man as if trying to resuscitate him. But now the Laird had risen and was moving rapidly toward the nearest door. In one thin hand he clutched a sheaf of papers.

Roy lurched forward drunkenly. He caught the escaping chief by the shoulder, spinning him around and snatching from him the little bundle of documents Macbeath had been carrying away.

"Thanks!" panted Garth, glancing more closely at the papers and then pocketing them. "It was good of you to find them for me. But I'll take care of them now. And of Stirling, too," he added, patting the collie's head. "I—"

His labored words died. Someone was coming in from the hall, the servants making way as she advanced. And now Garth and Kathleen were face to face once more, for the second time that day.

Even in her own room, at the far end of the castle, the girl had become aware at last of the unearthly noise, and she had come downstairs to learn its cause.

She gazed in bewilderment around the wrecked room and at the disheveled and panting man who stood swaying in its center.

"Roy!" she said, her voice muffled with wondering joy.

Then as she noted his tattered and wholly disreputable aspect, she ran up to him, crying:

"Oh, you're hurt—you're badly hurt! I—"

"My dear," interposed the Laird, his dry voice cutting like a rusty knife through her anxious exclamations, "you are wasting much good sympathy on quite the wrong man. If you can spare time from him to glance down there by the hearth, you will see the real object of solicitude. You will see also that a bottle of my most unprocurable Napoleon brandy has been broken by one or both of these earnest young gladiators—which places *me* in the sympathizable class, too."

Following his pointed finger's direction, Kathleen saw the giant body asprawl on the hearth. Roy stepped in front of her, to shield her from the gruesome sight.

"Let some of your men carry him to his room," Garth bade the Laird, "and get a doctor for him. Then may I trouble you to send the rest of the servants out of earshot? Unless you prefer to have them hear what must be said?"

Macbeath nodded in whimsical humility and rasped out a command or two. Presently the senseless Ulrich had been borne from the room and up the stairs to his own stuffy bedchamber. The last of the servants was gone and the study doors were closed.

"I am quite at your service," said Macbeath. "Your highness's orders have been obeyed. Up till this last week's American invasion I had formed a quaint Old World habit of giving all commands in my own castle. But I am learning. For example, here is your mightiness's mail, which arrived just ahead of you this evening. Will you deign to accept it?"

Ignoring the ponderous show of sarcasm and the low bow that accompanied it, Garth took the packet of half a dozen letters proffered him by the Laird and laid them on the table beside him.

"They can wait," he said without so much as a glance at any of them. "My business can't. So we'll attend to that, now, please."

Again Macbeath bowed low in ironic submission. Stirling had galloped over to Kathleen, and had greeted her tumultuously, after their four-day separation. Now he subsided, and the girl turned back to Garth.

"Roy," she pleaded, "what has happened? Tell me! Oh, I have been so horribly unhappy about you! Uncle told me about your escaping in that balloon and about its being seen above the North Sea. It's a golden miracle of God that you're—"

"If you will pardon my presumption in making a suggestion in my own house," said Macbeath, testily, "your rather maudlin remarks are interrupting Mr. Garth's so-called 'business.' And I am told that that is an unpardonable crime in his own poetic land. Pray proceed, Mr. Garth. My niece's hysterical interest in your adventures of the day is no more personal toward you than would be her sorrow over a dead pet cat. I hope you un-understand that clearly? Now as to your business—"

"Whatever your interest means, Kathleen," spoke up Garth, ignoring the Laird's sneer, "even if it is no more than it would be for a dead cat, as your uncle says, I am your lifelong grateful debtor for it. I want you to know that always."

He spoke from the heart, seeking only to keep his words as formally banal as their tone was ardent. He smiled into her troubled eyes; then he spoke again to the chief:

"I told your niece this morning the whole story of our deal about Stirling. I told her all of it. She believes me, and—"

"A woman usually believes anything an attractive man may tell her," observed Macbeath, dryly, "unless it chances to be true. The feminine heart is fearfully and wonderfully made. (So is the left hindleg of a camel.) Yes, I can well believe my credulous niece swallowed your entertaining fiction. Whether the law will be quite so gullible is another matter. Perhaps—"

"That is what I am coming to," answered Roy, keeping his temper and trying not to lose his eyes in Kathleen's. "I realize that in this corner of the Highlands you represent the law—or a travesty on it. Local constables are looking for me at this minute, and they are working overtime because Brant Ulrich offered them a thousand-dollar reward for laying me by the heels."

"Quite," cheerily assented Macbeath. "An excellent man of business, our possibly lamented friend, Ulrich. He—"

"You will send word—if you haven't already sent it —to tell them where to find me," proceeded Garth. "They will find me here and they will arrest me. They or others of your hangers-on will search me, on pretext of looking for concealed weapons. They will have orders from you to take and then 'lose' the bunch of papers that prove my ownership of Stirling here."

"You are a mind-reader!" exclaimed Macbeath with real admiration. "That is precisely what they will do. In which case you will merely be a lawbreaking foreigner with not one shred of evidence to back your cock-and-bull story of having bought Stirling. Meanwhile I shall make out a new set of papers—for Glamis. These will be found among your luggage and will—"

"No," contradicted Roy. "I think you're mistaken.

You've overlooked the one important item in the whole sorry affair."

Turning again to Kathleen, he drew out the little sheaf of transfer papers and handed them to her.

"You have heard the pleasant trick your uncle is planning to play," said he. "Everything hangs on this packet's safety and on its being kept as evidence for me. I am going to ask you to keep it. I know you won't let anyone bully you or cajole you or threaten you into giving it up. Will you keep it safe for me, Kathleen, till I can get hold of a reliable lawyer and send him to you for it? Will you?"

With no word of reply, the girl looked long and silently at him, then at her saturninely smiling uncle. Then she took the sheaf from Roy's hand and hid it in the breast of her dinner frock.

Garth drew a long breath, his light eyes misting.

"I knew I could trust you," he said, quietly, but with all his heart and soul in his gaze.

"Mr. Garth," broke in Macbeath, his gaunt body shaken with unwonted laughter, "I did you a rank injustice a few minutes ago. I began to think you were a man of intelligence. I see I was wrong. My apologies. You are the silly fool I took you for at the outset. That is the American of it. They tell me Americans are hard as nails in business, but soft as mush with their women. You have proved it. You had one card left in your hand— your ace of trumps. It would have won the game, in spite of my excellent bluffing. And you have thrown it away—thrown it straight into your opponent's hand."

"I think not," said Garth, his eyes still on Kathleen's.

"It is a matter of easy proof!" answered Macbeath. "Here in the Highlands our women still obey us, as nature intended woman to obey man. They obey us as implicitly as our collies. For example: Kathleen, you will take those documents our quixotic young friend has just been fool enough to give you and you will carry them at once to my safe. You know the combination. You will lock them in there. Then you will go to bed. That is all. Good night."

Kathleen's gaze still held Garth's as her uncle spoke. But now the brown eyes were inscrutable and there was a glint of pain in them. Without a word she went to the doorway. With no backward look she passed out through it. ·

"You see!" chuckled Macbeath. "Now do you care to stay here until the constables come for you? It won't be long. I cannot offer you a drink, thanks to the careless smashing of my last hoarded bottle of eighteen-hundred-and-ten Napoleon brandy. But—"

"Thanks," assented Roy. "I'll stay. Not till the police come, but until Miss Macbeath comes back. It will be only a few minutes."

"I did not ask you to stay here until morning," corrected the Laird, "and my niece will not return until then. You heard me tell her to lock those papers carefully in my safe and then go to bed."

Roy shrugged his shoulders. To pass the time, sooner

than remain in talk with his host, he reached for the packet of letters Macbeath had handed him and which he had laid on the table. He shuffled the envelopes, glancing at their superscriptions. All were from Midwestburg. One was sprawlingly addressed in Jamie Mackellar's hand. One, apparently, was from Belden himself. Three were bills. The sixth was in Phyllis's ultramodern chirography.

It was Garth's first letter from his fiancée since he had left home. Morbidly he wondered why he had not the faintest interest in opening it. Urging himself by a sense of duty, he tore the envelope and pulled forth the folded sheet it contained. Before he could open the page a growl of astonished wrath from Macbeath made him glance up.

Kathleen stood in the doorway.

"I told you to go to bed as soon as you put those things in the safe!" roared the chief, glowering menacingly at her. "I don't wish you to remain in the same room with this bounder. Be off!"

She flinched. But instead of departing, she walked up to her uncle.

"I did not put them in the safe, sir," she said, frightened but with her sweet voice firm and quiet. "I hid them—somewhere else, where neither you nor anyone but myself can ever find them until Roy sends to me for them. I am sorry, but there was nothing else to do."

The Laird was on his feet, ghastly white, his black old eyes aflame, his mouth working convulsively, his gaunt frame aquiver. He strove to speak, but he seemed to be strangling. He could only gurgle as he shook his clawlike fists at the shrinking girl.

"Thank you a million times," Roy was saying to her. "I knew you wouldn't betray me. I—"

"Betray!" spat Macbeath, catching at the word. "*Betray!* She has played the petticoat Judas to *me*—to the man who—"

"No, sir," denied Kathleen, facing him now unafraid. "That is not true. I should have been betraying you hideously if I let you do what you were planning to—if I let my own uncle—the chief of my own clan—sink to theft and to defrauding a guest. It would have been the blackest smirch on our house since King Macbeth murdered his sovereign and stole his throne. According to our code, we have been honest—we have been honorable—we Macbeaths—for centuries and centuries. It would have been wicked betrayal of you and of your own standards if I had let you do this abominable thing. I—"

"You—you betrayed me for this Yankee imbecile!" mouthed her uncle, flecks of foam on his thin lips. "You love him! That is why. *You love him!*"

He fairly screeched the accusation at her, as though it were foul.

"Macbeath!" cried Garth in warning; seeking to protect the girl from mortification, his own heart hammering crazily as he spoke.

"*You love him!*" raved her uncle again. "You love—"

"Yes," Kathleen made amazing answer, speaking with entire calmness, but letting her dark eyes rest tenderly on

Roy's quivering face. "Yes, I do. I love him with all my heart, Uncle. And I am very sure indeed that he loves me. You do, don't you, Roy?" she finished, with the terrible directness of a little child as she came close to him and looked up into his tortured eyes.

"You do, don't you, dear?" she repeated, confidently.

Garth's tortured soul clamored crazily to him to catch her in his arms and to tell her she was all the world and all of heaven and hell to him, and that there could never again be another woman but herself in his life.

Then Phyllis Belden's letter seemed to burn into his palm as he clenched spasmodically the hand that held it.

Phyllis Belden, the fly-away girl of his earlier infatuation, the daintily fluff-brained young woman whom propinquity and enforced secrecy and difference in worldly station had made so supremely desirable to him! Compared to Kathleen, she was a futile shadow. Yet his word and his faith were pledged to her.

Because of that pledged word he must push aside the most divine cup of perfect happiness that life could hold to the lips of mortal man. Glorious love here was his for the taking. And he must needs pass it by—for the sake of a flighty and shallow-hearted girl for whom he could no longer care.

The future stretched out before him, dreary and barren as a rainy sea. He had won his quest. He had achieved his difficult mission. He had played at dice with death. With his naked hands he had crushed the rival who sought to outwit him and to kill him. By brains and by fierce courage and by luck he had bested also this super-crafty Scotsman who had schemed his undoing.

He had triumphed. He had won the right to go back and to claim Phyllis as the prize of his victory! And he would have given his life right blithely for the right to draw this sweeter and deeper and lovelier and honester Scottish girl into his arms for one heavenly minute!

Yet he must shame Kathleen cruelly by refusing the wonder-gift she was proffering to him. That was the keenest anguish of all. Roy felt as though he were about to dash his fist into the smiling face of some child who loved and trusted him.

He could see the tender light in Kathleen's eyes merge into troubled wonder as he made no reply to her glorious declaration. And still he could only stare down miserably and wordlessly at her. It was Macbeath who broke the stark silence.

"Ma certie!" roared the Laird, in high-pitched gleeful malevolence. "The cad will have none of you, lassie! D'ye see that? He's refusing you! 'Twas easy, and 'twas monstrous good fun, for him to make love to you, for the sake of prying out where Stirling was hid. He's made your loyalty turn to him from your own flesh and blood. But now that he's got what he wants from us—"

"That's not true!" flashed Kathleen. "You shan't say it is! Roy, *tell* him he is misjudging you! *Tell* him, my beloved!"

With something like a groan Roy Garth turned away, unable to bear the trusting look in her face. He moved blindly back toward the table, like a drunkard. His hand gripped the crumpled letter from Phyllis Belden as though it were the throat of a mortal enemy.

Then, as a cranky child bites on a sore tooth to make it hurt worse, deliberately Garth yanked wide the rumpled page and forced his sick brain to concentrate on it.

What had he to do with the Highland girl who was weeping, so close behind him, or with the sardonic old man whose high-pitched guffaws filled the dusty room? He was engaged to Phyllis Belden. He had won her for his wife.

He held in his bleeding hand the first love letter Phyllis had ever written him. By all means, he must read it! It was a fit climax to everything. With teeth set and heart dead, the man glanced loathingly at the page he had smoothed out.

Roy, [the letter began], *you won't like this. But medicine is best without sugar in it. You left for Scotland last night. I lay awake nearly a whole hour after I went to bed, thinking of that ghastly last evening we spent here together. Then I got to wondering how long I could keep from dying of boredom if I had to spend such evenings with you all my whole life long. And that gave me the answer.*

I think we thought we were crazy about each other, because it was such fun to carry on an engagement right under dad's very nose without his finding it out or threatening to shoot you. Then when we found he really knew, all the time, and that he didn't mind a bit, and that it was all humdrum and aboveboard—well, that just about makes the whole thing as flat as one of Brant Ulrich's jokes.

At least it does so far as I am concerned, and I'm the only one I'm concerned about.

I can't marry you, Roy. There's the whole of it in five words. I'm sick of—

"May I venture to interrupt your epistolary labors, Mr. Garth," Macbeath's file-rasping voice broke in on Roy's dazed perusal, "so far as to ask you for the second time to leave my house before I have you kicked out? The air will be cleaner to breathe when—"

Roy heard no more. He woke from his trance of rapturous wonder, to see the Laird scowling down at him. Kathleen had left the room. He caught a flutter of her white dress in the passage beyond.

In two bounds Garth had reached the passageway; he had caught up with the drooping figure, gathering it into his arms, crushing it close to his heart, blurting out insensate love words, trying to tell the girl a hundred times at once, how God-givenly glorious she was and how utterly he worshiped her.

Out into the passage after him strode Macbeath, declaiming, harshly:

"I forbid you to speak to my niece again! You will leave this house immediately and—"

His thunderous speech of dismissal ceased abruptly as

he came into view of the man and the maid. The Laird
made a queer gobbling sound such as might be voiced
by a turkey whose tail feathers are pulled. He stood for
a few seconds with eyes abulge. Then, his gaunt body
swaying, he turned about and stumbled feebly back into
the disordered study.

The lovers had not so much as heard Macbeath's bel-
lowed denunciation, nor known he had followed them
into the passage.

They did not guess nor care that a beaten old man was
crouching now in front of his dying study fire, muttering
noiseless words to the embers, while the great collie at
his side strove wistfully to comfort him.

"But—but, sweetheart," asked Kathleen at last, "why
didn't you answer me right away? Why did you let me
feel as if the whole world had all come to an end? *Why*
did you, Roy?"

"Perhaps," answered Garth, foolish with happiness—
"perhaps I was afraid if I spoke I'd—I'd wake up. Shan't
we let it go at that, girl of my heart? Nothing else matters, any more, except just—just us!"